The Floater

In The Kill

Will Allyn

Order this book online at www.trafford.com
or email orders@trafford.com

Most Trafford titles are also available at major online book retailers.

Note for Librarians: A cataloguing record for this book is available from Library
and Archives Canada at www.collectionscanada.ca/amicus/index-e.html

Printed in Victoria, BC, Canada.

ISBN: 9781-4269-023-5-2 (soft)
ISBN: 9781-4269-023-6-9 (hard)
ISBN: 9781-4269-023-7-6 (eBook)

*Our mission is to efficiently provide the world's finest, most comprehensive
book publishing service, enabling every author to experience success.
To find out how to publish your book, your way, and have it available*

Trafford rev. 8/20/09

 www.trafford.com

North America & international
toll-free: 1 888 232 4444 (USA & Canada)
phone: 250 383 6864 ♦ fax: 812 355 4082

Acknowledgements

My thanks to my family and friends whose encouragement helped produce this book:

To my wife, Pat, and my brother Bob and his wife, Doris; my good friends, Elinor, Irma, Dave, Patty, and Larry and my writer's workshop cohorts, Lois and Chris - first readers and critics all.

Special thanks to Kean University professors James Connor and Henry Hocherman whose exhortations "dare to be great" still resound.

Prologue

The place stank. It was 2:30 of a hot August Sunday morning, a half hour after the liquor law in Linden, NJ dictated the close of all bars. Stale cigarette smoke, ashtrays filled with stubbed cigarettes, the stale dregs of six ounce beer glasses, whiskey soaked bar rags and the curious odor of cheap perfume permeated the place. The miasma of spiced food and day old fish from the kitchen added to the stagnant atmosphere. The barroom was dark except for the light from the partially open kitchen door and two overhead lights that illuminated the far end of the oval mahogany bar where the three sat - Al Dalton, the owner of The Haunt, Ben Chusinsky, one of his bar managers, and Margarita Garcia, Ben's current squeeze, who sat between them. A sullenness rose into the strata of gray and blue Marlboro smoke that hung ominously above them. All was not well.

"Ben, don't fuck with me. I want the bread and I want it now. Two big ones. You got yours, didn't ya?" snarled Al.

"Al, gimme some time, will ya?"

"Time I ain't got and neither do you. I give ya a chance to make a coupla bucks and ya screw me."

"Whadaya mean, ya gimme a chance? It was your shit I was peddlin', right outta your own place and you're givin' me the heat?"

Ben was getting agitated. He had been selling coke and grass for Dalton so Al wouldn't get caught with it. Some of the customers were Al's and now Al was giving him a hard time because they didn't or wouldn't pay up on time.

"It's a cash business and I told ya so. No cash, no shit. I gotta pay up front on my end and I ain't lettin' nothin' hang outta my pocket. You been into me for months now. You knew the score when your girlfriend here brought you in. Ya been peddlin' before. Ya needed a pad, I gave ya one upstairs. Ya needed a coupla bucks, I gave it to ya. Ya needed some quick cash, I let ya in on it," Dalton was screaming.

A huge ego and years of swilling beer, boiler makers, snorting cocaine and smoking marijuana had taken its toll on Dalton. His brains were fried and he rose easily to anger and violent rage. "Now, I want the cash and I want it here one o'clock this afternoon. You dig? Two grand, asshole. Now beat it."

Margarita glanced uneasily from one to the other and back; a ping pong conversation, the slams harder, more vicious with each volley. She moved to Ben's left away from Dalton. She knew Dalton when he had other bars and it was she who introduced Ben to him. She had seen Al in fits of rage, seen him whack a street dealer with a ball bat, nearly killing him and then throwing him out of the bar into the street.

She tugged at Ben's sleeve. "Come on, Ben. Honey, let's go."

Dalton couldn't contain himself. "Honey? Margie, this guy ain't worth a shit. Get yourself a man."

Chusinsky slid from his stool and grabbed Dalton by the throat. "Ya wanna repeat that, ya dumb fuck?"

Dalton twisted free and leaped to the kitchen and grabbed a knife from the counter. Cat-like he sprang back through the door slashing the air. Ben backed off and found himself trapped with his back against the bar. The knife arced downward as Ben raised his left arm to fend off the blow. The adrenalin of pain brought him to the edge of frenzy. He grasped his arm and felt the blood and the open wound. He spun away to his right but Dalton was on him like a panther, stabbing him in the back. Pain seared Ben's brain and he turned again to disarm Dalton, to get away, to do anything to avoid the slashing knife. Now Dalton grinned. He sneered at the hapless figure facing him and plunged the knife upward into his chest. Ben gasped and fell forward, arms instinctively around Dalton's waist, his shoulder against Al's stomach. Dalton stabbed Ben in the back again and again until he was exhausted. He stepped aside and Chusinsky fell forward, dead before he hit the floor.

Margarita stood pale and shaking, her fist in her mouth, a scream stuck in her throat.

Silence engulfed them, heavy and oppressive. Dalton surveyed the scene. Blood oozed from beneath the body, blood spatters on the bar, the floor, his clothes, Margarita's dress, on the wall behind him.

Dalton took Margarita by one arm, squeezed, twisted and raised her to her toes. His six feet towered over her petite five foot two inch frame. "One word outta you and they'll ship your body back to Colombia. Comprende?"

Margarita shook her head in horrified silence, her hand over her mouth. She backed out of the room through the emergency exit, turned and fled.

Chapter One

8:00 am - Monday, August 11th
The Arthur Kill

The early morning sun burned from a cloudless sky glinting from the tops of the early morning wavelets in the Arthur Kill. Jake Harney strolled along the gravelly Elizabeth shoreline of the tidal channel between New Jersey and New York connecting Newark Bay with Raritan Bay. He listened to the fascinating but ominous chirping of cicadas and squinted against the sequined, incoming tide. He looked across the half mile width to Staten Island and breathed deeply at the fresh, briny air. But the Thursday morning sun and cicadas warned of another one of those sultry dog days of August. Jake liked these early morning walks. They were refreshing; cleared his sotted head, and gave Jocko a chance to run before being leashed for the day to his dog house in the yard. Jocko liked it, too. A Collie and Shepherd mix, he leaped from the ripples as they washed against the sand and debris of the busy industrial waterway and chased them as they washed back into the murky depths. Sometimes he would play tag with the swells of the wake of a tug pushing an oil barge to one of the refineries down stream.

This morning he held his nose high to the onshore breeze, pranced circles in front of Jake begging for the routine game of fetch with a piece of flotsam that would be thrown for him to chase. Jake obliged and flung a piece of driftwood as far as he could. Jocko's head whirled as he watched it arc overhead and land in a splash of sand and water at the shoreline. His fur rose and fell with each leap as he bounded after it. He took it in his mouth and flipped it in the air to catch it further back in his jaws to shake the water from it. Trotting back, he braked to a stop and dropped the stick in front of a white plastic wrapped bundle as it heaved and sagged in the rise and fall of muddied water. He yapped at it, pawed and snapped at it and danced back and forth, to and fro between the lapping and receding swells of a passing tug. The bundle refused to play and Jocko sat, barking and looking from bundle to Jake, Jake to bundle.

"Now what did you find?" laughed Jake. He approached the bundle and quickly took mental measurements: about six feet long, three feet across and tapered from one end to the other. Gray duct tape was wrapped tightly around the bundle. He gulped. "Let's go, Jocko. Here, boy. Jocko, let's go!"

With Jocko at his heels, he sprinted as well as a fifty six year old could. He stopped, panting at the phone at the end of the abandoned pier. Trembling, he tried to push the touchtone buttons with an uncontrollable finger. He stopped, inhaled deeply, held his breath to keep from shaking, and dialed 911.

Chapter Two

10:30 am - Monday, August 11th
The Office of the State Medical Examiner

The room was cavernous. Lined with white tile, it echoed every sound, every word. Five stainless steel autopsy tables lined the back wall; all occupied and in varying stages of a post mortem. Forensic pathologists deftly sliced their way to critical organs, taking cross section samples, weighing them, placing them in formaldehyde and dictating notes into the overhead microphones. Deaners assisted the pathologists, weighing and preparing the body, taking full length color photographs of the corpses and close-ups of critical areas, draining the table of body fluids, closing and sewing the cadavers' opened chests.

Detective Sergeant Andrew Sutton, Elizabeth, NJ, Police Department, stared at the bundle in front of him. Strips of duct tape held the bundle together while an orange colored outdoor electrical extension cord spiraled the entire assembly. A blue floral print comforter hung from the lower end. Still soggy and wet, the assortment lay on the tilted table begging to be opened and examined.

"Excuse me, Drew," the voice of Jerry Miner jarred Sutton from his contemplation. "I need to get in there and take a couple of flics."

"Sure. Sure." Drew gave way and watched as Jerry took full length photos, close ups of knots in the extension cord and wrappings of silver duct tape. "This thing been x-rayed yet?"

"Yeah. They waited for me before they did. Nothing showed." Jerry was the department's better crime scene examiner and photographer. Didn't miss much, if anything, and was always thinking; always one step ahead.

"Great, Jerry. Make two sets of prints, will you? One set for evidence and one for me."

"What're ya gonna do, hang 'em in the shithouse?"

"Yeah," Drew was in no mood for jokes. He caught this job only because he took Jackie Ryan's call and began to regret it. "Hang around, pinhead. We'll need you when we unwrap Poseidon's gift."

The unmistakable odor of a decomposing body attacked their nostrils. The dog days of August in New Jersey was not the time to catch a "floater" Sutton thought. Some said to smoke a cigar. Others said to burn coffee grounds in a pot. Drew thought they all didn't know what the hell they were talking about. Nothing stinks like a rotting corpse and nothing can cover it up. This floater was a little different. Its immersion in water for however long seemed to delay decomposition. Patrol and the Crime Scene Unit had done a good job in preserving the scene with the ubiquitous yellow police tape and a quick response by the Medical Examiner's investigators had spared the corpse from the summer sun and heat. This was going to be a real whodunit and this early autopsy would help.

Drew raised his eyes at the sound of the hissing automatic door. Dr. Ariella Serfis, M.E. strode to the table and nodded to Drew.

"Well, Sergeant, we meet again."

"You say that every time, Doc."

She was Chief Pathologist of the State's Northern Regional Laboratory and permitted few to address her as "Doc." Drew was different. More than once his critical eye caught a clue when they went over her findings as the deaner closed up. And she liked the six foot two frame that rippled under his shirt. More than once they sat side by side in the conference room going over pictures and notes, studying the death certificate and its blocks for the findings of the cause and manner of death. And more than once their elbows touched with neither moving away. But the subject at hand always seemed to divert whatever attraction might have developed

"And where did you find this one?"

"In the Arthur Kill."

"What the hell is a Kill?"

"It's a Dutch name; means river, channel or creek."

"Not that it matters," said the pathologist.

"Not to him, anyway," retorted Drew.

"All right, let's unwrap it."

"George," she shouted to the Deaner working at the next table. "Put on a new pair of gloves and help me here."

Carefully they removed the comforter and extension cord and spread them out on an adjoining table. The cord had been cut and a piece appeared missing. The soggy comforter was intact. No manufacturer's tag was present. Nor was there any identifying tag on the cord. Jerry photoed them both and placed them in separate boxes, labeling them as evidence with time and date.

Dr. Serfis cut the plastic wrapping up the front from toe to head with surgical scissors. It too was photoed and placed in an evidence box. Detective Miner took photographs of the body. Bloody fluids had oozed onto the plastic.

"Looks like a male, folks," Jerry grinned and glanced at Dr. Serfis.

Ariella caught his snicker. "How would you know?"

"Jerry, take his prints and clippings and let's get on with it, OK?" Drew interjected. Jerry's big fault was his sorry sense of humor.

Jerry took fingerprints and fingernail clippings. The clippings were placed in envelopes marked LT, LI, LM, LR and LP. The same for the right hand. On his left ring finger was found a black onyx ring. Pictures were taken and the ring cut off. No inscription was found but the cameo of a white knight's head was on the onyx.

The forensic pathologist examined the ring and made a mental note of it.

No markings except a puncture stab wound in the upper left torso and a wound on the back of the left arm were noted.

"Turn him over, George," the M.E. directed.

The corpse was turned on its right side. More bloody fluid oozed onto the table from eleven stab wounds to the back.

"Shoot these, Detective Miner," growled Ariella, "and you can leave."

Miner placed a six inch ruler above or below each wound for reference, took the pictures, picked up the evidence boxes and slipped from the room.

"Okay, Drew, here we go. Hand me the Deaner's notes over there, will you?" She pulled the overhead mike to her and intoned her preliminary notes:

"The body is that of a Caucasian male, one hundred ninety three pounds, five feet ten inches tall. The fingernails have been clipped by Detective Miner. A black onyx ring with a knight's head has been removed from the left ring finger leaving a circular mark. Removal was made by Detective Miner by cutting the ring from the finger. There is a lateral wound on the posterior aspect of the left forearm measuring three inches located six inches below the cubitus. The body shows marked symptoms of immersion. Rigor is absent. There is a lateral wound measuring one and one quarter inches penetrating the left thorax two inches below the sternum and two and one half inches to the left. The wound appears to have been made in an upward thrust."

"I think he had a heart attack, Doc." Drew's attempt at levity was met with a cold silence.

"He should have been so lucky," she retorted. "The poor bastard bled out."

"Well, Doc, I'm on my way. I've seen all I need to know to get started on this." Drew started toward the door. "Can you rush your protocol?" He tossed the request over his shoulder.

"As soon as I can, Detective. You're fifth in line."

"Can you tell me how long he's been dead?"

"I'll tell you that when you tell me who the last person was to see him alive."

"You always say that, Doc."

"Not staying for the close?"

"Not this time, Doc. You don't need me and I have to find out who 'poor bastard' is so I can find out who killed him." Drew scooted out the door and quickly stuck his head back in. "Call me if you need me."

Doctor Serfis raised an undetected eyebrow.

Chapter Three

7:00 am - Tuesday - August 14th
Elizabeth Police Headquarters

This morning was a contemplative moment for Sergeant Sutton. He sat at the shoreline of the Kill on a beached piece of creosoted piling. Pieces of the ubiquitous yellow police tape still fluttered from the poles and debris to which they had been attached. He sat poking at the sand oblivious to the chugging of a laboring tug, unmindful of the mixed smell of oil and salt on a fair onshore breeze. It was three days since the body had been found and he had convinced Bobby Mercer, the police reporter, to run a release on the homicide with special emphasis on the ring. I.D. had submitted the prints to the State Police for comparison and he had searched the **N**ational **C**rime **I**nformation **C**enter for missing persons. Yet as relentless as he was in pursuit of the truth; as logical and imaginative as he was; it was all up to forensics now. He could do nothing more than wait.

He sat watching the current of the tidal river, gauging its direction and speed. A squawking sea-gull rocked to a landing in front of him, a strand of yellow crime scene tape clinging to his left leg. He was an odd looking bird; white head and body with black wings edged in white. He looked as if he were wearing a tuxedo. They eyed each other. *All right, Tuxedo, where were you when they dumped the body* he muttered to the gull -- *want to tell me about it?* The gull cocked his head, flapped his wings and soared above him, wheeling, dipping, squealing and squawking as if it were crying for understanding, the yellow ribbon trailing behind like a biplane towed banner. *I'm going nuts,* he thought. *I swear the damn thing winked at me.*

He looked at his watch and looked downstream. Here he comes and right on time Sutton thought and got up to greet Jake Harney. He had interviewed him early on and liked the old man who had an air of hard knocks and common sense about him.

"Morning, Mr. Harney. See you and Jocko doing your usual morning thing."

"Yep." nodded Harney. A further glance brightened his face. "Well, howdy, Detective. Didn't recognize you at first. Watcha doin' here?"

"Looking."

"For what?"

"Anything, something, nothing," grinned Sutton. "How long have you been walking the Kill?"

"'Bout nine years; ever since I moved into town. Great mornin' picker-upper."

"Always the same time?"

"Yep. Gotta get to work, you know," responded Harney.

"I'm looking at the current," Sutton mused. "Which way is it flowing?"

"Well, right now it's runnin' from south to north. You know, from down Linden way to Newark Bay."

"Flows that way all the time this time of the morning?"

"Yep. Pretty much. The tide time table ain't the same all the time, of course. But if you're askin' me which way the body come from, it floated up from Linden way," crowed Harney.

"You'd swear to that in court?"

Harney's face clouded. "You're not gonna make me get up in court, are you?"

Sutton smiled. He recognized the reluctance of someone who had gone through the judicial process before - on the other side. "No, no. Just testing. Wanted to see how certain you were."

Jocko galloped over and tugged at Harney's sleeve.

"Gotta go," Harney said, relieved at the interruption.

Sutton waved and headed for his car. "Thanks, Mr. Harney. Thanks for your time and conversation."

"Don't mention it."

Sutton walked toward the road. Dammit he muttered. How the hell am I going to do anything with this leaking bag of shit? A body - no name. A killing - no weapon. A crime - no suspect. No forensics, no nothing. And now I've got to listen to Lt. Traxel.

Det/Sgt Sutton poked his head around the half open door to Lt. Bernie Traxel's office.

"You wanted to see me, Boss?"

Traxel looked up from his pile of papers.

"Sure. Just give me a couple of minutes while I unscramble this report. Grab a coffee in the conference room and pour me one. Dark, no sugar," replied the Lieutenant.

Sutton felt relieved. An invitation to the conference room usually meant a casual discussion of something or another. A talk in his office usually meant a "counseling", something he didn't need at this moment. Sutton had poured the coffee when Traxel walked in.

"How was the day off?" Traxel asked. "Do anything exciting?"

"Nah. Just hung out. Running this floater thing through my mind."

"Look," Traxel responded, "I've redistributed your case load. You're on this thing full time for a week. And you can pick a partner. How about Jackie Ryan? It was his call you took."

Sutton's jaw dropped. "Why? There's nothing to work on right now. It's a dead end until we find out who he is."

"That's true. His name was Benjamin Chusinsky."

"How the hell did you find that out?" pleaded Sutton.

Traxel pushed an NCIC printout across the table. "They got a hit on his prints yesterday. He's out of Perth Amboy. Got a nickname of Big Ben. A couple of possession arrests. Lost his license for about six months last year for driving under the influence. Checked his address. People say he moved out over a year ago - don't know where to. Post Office has no forwarding address."

"Okay. Okay. How about me and Eddy Nolan?"

"That's what I said. Eddy Nolan." Traxel laughed. He knew enough to let the guys chose their partners. "By the way, Dr. Serfis called, wants to talk to you. Any idea what about?" His eyes scanned Sutton's face and saw nothing.

"Beats me, Lieu. When did she call?"

"Yesterday. And Drew, come up with something on this, will you? The Chief was asking about it."

Sutton and Nolan were going over notes on the case when Irene, one of the Detective Bureau's secretaries, walked up.

"Drew, there's a Mr. and Mrs. Michael Chusinsky outside. Want to talk to you. Her name is Susan." She waited for instructions.

Sutton and Nolan looked at each other. "Ask them into the interview room, will you, Irene? Tell them we'll be right in."

"Grab the ring and the head shot, Eddy. This may be our break."

They looked at the pair through the one - way glass in the wall of the interview room. The couple were about sixty five years old but looked more. Mrs. Chusinsky appeared the typical old - country housewife, whose only focus in life was to keep a clean house, serve good meals to her working husband and keep the children safe and educated. Her lined face showed the strain of that life - wrinkled and settled under a halo of gray hair nestled in a summer straw. Seated, she appeared to be about five feet five inches tall and showing a plumpness from eating her own good cooking. Her dish-pan hands were clasped in front of her on the table, at times twisting the skirt of her red and blue summer dress.

Mr. Chusinsky sat stolidly beside her, looking straight ahead. Dressed in a suit and tie that had been bought on 14th Street in New York City some years prior, he looked more like a shoe store proprietor than the machinist he was. What his wife lacked in height he made up in his six foot spare frame. They didn't hold hands, speak or touch each other. There were no outward signs of endearment but Drew could sense their warmth for each other; an affection and support annealed in the fire of hard times.

Drew and Eddy entered and introduced themselves. "Hi. Mr. and Mrs. Chusinsky?"

They nodded wordlessly.

"I'm Sergeant Sutton and this is my partner Detective Nolan. How can we help?" The detectives sat on one side of them at the round table - a feature introduced by Lt. Traxel to avoid a confrontational setting.

Mrs. Chusinsky straightened in her chair. "We read the paper about the man in the river and his ring."

Drew and Eddy squirmed a little. Regardless of the number of times done, death notification was always difficult. But it came with the territory; part of the job.

Mrs. Chusinsky continued, "My son, Benny, he's been missing for about ten days. He has a ring like the one in the paper."

She fidgeted. Her body language said let's get on with it. Her eyes pleaded in denial. Her use of the present tense did not escape Sutton.

Drew nodded to Eddy.

"Can you describe the ring, Mrs. Chusinsky?"

"It's a black onyx with a white knights head on it," interrupted Mr. Chusinsky. "We gave it to him when he graduated high school." He looked knowingly at the detectives. Let's get on with it, his eyes said.

"Is this the ring?" proffered Eddy.

Mrs. Chusinsky sagged in her chair, her face cupped in her leathered hands.

Mr. Chusinsky took the ring and turned it over and over like a jeweler making an appraisal. "That's it." Stoically he handed it to Drew.

How many times have they been through situations with their son, Drew wondered. "Mr. Chusinsky," Drew asked, "Would you mind looking at a photograph of the man that was wearing this ring?"

Chusinsky nodded and Eddy handed him the photo taken at the autopsy. He stared at the photo of the bloated face. "Looks like him."

"Can you be sure?"

"It's probably him."

"We need to have someone go with us to the morgue to make a positive identification. I'd rather it not be you two. You've gone through enough already. Is there someone else at home?"

"My other son, Norman, is waiting in the car downstairs. He drove us here."

"All right, sir. But before we go we need to ask a few more questions. Do you mind?"

"No."

Drew asked, "Tell us where you live."

"1170 Broad Lawn Boulevard, Perth Amboy."

"Broad Lawn?"

"Yes, you know; must have named the street when there were lawns. But not now. Everything's too crowded for lawns, broad ones anyway." Chusinsky chuckled a bit.

Drew was relieved at the old man's attempt at levity.

"When was the last time you saw Benjamin?"

"About ten, eleven days ago. He has a small apartment above us. Been living there about a year after he had his license revoked. I drove him to work every now and then when he needed a ride. He worked at a bar; a saloon in Linden called the "Haunt". A go-go thing where the girls dance. He helps out with the books, was a bookkeeper once. The last I saw him was when I dropped him off about ten at night on August 3rd.

"He never came home after that," Mrs. Chusinsky sobbed. "He would come and see me for breakfast or for a late bite sometimes. Nothing like that since Michael dropped him off."

"Did he ever have any visitors at the apartment?" asked Sutton.

"Yes. A couple of girls, you know - the dancers."

"Know who they are?"

"No. But I have the license plates of the cars that were parked outside. You know, they would drive him home and stay awhile. I don't have them here. They're home."

"Good, Mrs. Chusinsky. We'll come down about noon. Now let's talk to Norman. We'll have one of the detectives drive you home and Norman and we will go to the morgue," Drew responded

"And I'm sorry for your loss," consoled Eddy.

"Thank you, Detective. But I have to tell you - about seven days ago when I got really worried, I called The Haunt and asked for Benny. Some man answered and got real nasty. He shouted who are you the morgue? That's when I really got worried."

Sergeant Sutton's heart pounded.

Broadlawn Boulevard in Perth Amboy was one of those neat, one block long streets lined with one and a half story red brick bungalows that some real estate agent would call a "real nice mother daughter combination." The home at 1170 had been a "mother- son "; the son's part being a three room apartment under the gable roof. Mrs. Chusinsky met Sutton and Nolan at the door before they could ring the bell. "Please come in," she whispered.

They walked in the small vestibule at the foot of the stairs to the second floor. Mr. Chusinsky sat in the dining room off to the left at the round oak table staring straight ahead. He did not acknowledge them. Mrs. Chusinsky led them silently up the stairs and opened the door to what had been Ben Chusinsky's home; a typical man's apartment - living room, kitchen, bedroom and bath; not that well kept. A cursory look around the rooms produced nothing of evidentiary or forensic value. Chusinsky was one of those men who wanted nothing and kept nothing. No packets of letters; no diary; and surprisingly, no book of telephone numbers. The court suspension order of his driving privileges was tucked into the frame of his bedroom mirror in an effort, the detectives surmised, to remind him of the expiration of the order and the restoration of his license.

Mrs. Chusinsky explained he had lived there for about a year and half but had not paid them any rent for over six months. Ben had been very secretive and did not divulge much of his personal life. Sometimes he would be gone two or three days without leaving word as to what he was doing or where he was doing it. He had, at one time, worked for a chain of used car repair and service lots before the job at the bar.

"What did he do at the Haunt?" asked Nolan.

"I really don't know," she said, "He said something about being a manager."

"Was he happy there? Did he make a good salary?" queried Sutton.

"I can't help you," she whimpered.

"Did he ever say anything about a problem at the bar?"

"Never."

"You mentioned a couple of girlfriends that came to the house. Tell us about them," Sutton urged.

"There's not much to tell. When he did have company, he would leave a sign on his door saying he had company. That meant don't come up. So I never really got a good look at any of his girlfriends or talk to them."

"You mentioned something about license plates."

"Yes. I don't know why but I took them down when I made breakfast for Michael and saw them parked in front of the house. Here they are."

Mrs. Chusinsky held out the paper to Drew, her lip and chin quivering. Drew stepped toward her to take it when she burst into tears and clutched at him, her head against his chest and arms around his waist. "My Benny, my Benny," she sobbed. "Please find whoever did this. Please."

Drew instinctively did what he had done often when his mother needed support; he held her.

Eddy Nolan turned away. He had two sons of his own; much younger but sons nevertheless. He headed for the stairs.

Drew extracted himself from the pathetic woman and followed. He turned and looked at her. "I will," he murmured. "We'll do our best."

Chapter Four

10:00 Am - Friday, August 15th
The Haunt

Sutton and Nolan got out of their nondescript unmarked car in front of 125 Woodmere Rd., Linden, New Jersey and approached the front door of "The Haunt". Years prior the building had been a store front with an apartment above. Now the once glass store front was bricked up with a row of thin windows above. Above the windows a sign was the only indication of a bar; "The Haunt" the first line said. And below, "Continuous Go-Go Dancing." The paint on the weather boards peeled in large hanging flakes adding to the desolate appearance of the place. But there was nothing mysterious about it. It was a gin mill; a gin mill with half naked girls gyrating around brass poles. Some were good looking. There were two doors in the brick front -- a sun faded brown door to the left and a grimy white, weather streaked door to the right of the brown one near the middle of the building. Experience told them the left most door led up a flight of stairs to an upstairs apartment. Nolan knocked on the white one. No answer. Sutton slammed the palm of his hand on the door a couple of times. "That'll wake up the dead," he muttered. Still no answer.

Nolan grinned. "Maybe the dead are deaf."

Sutton jiggled the loose and cracked brass door knob and pushed in. "It's a public establishment," he said. "We're customers, right?" Sutton led the way in down a dim aisle ~~formed~~ by a wall on his left and a long oval bar on his right. Bar stools stood in disarray forcing them to dodge each like a slow motion broken field running back. Stale cigarette smoke and the stench of beer glasses in varying degrees of emptiness poked at their noses. Ahead, at the end of the bar, was the shadow of a man hunched over a card table. A green shaded lamp hung over the table and light streaming from the open door on the left gave him the specter of a scene in an Alfred Hitchcock movie. Startled, he dropped his pencil on the open ledger and threw a newspaper over the cash drawer as the detectives approached.

"We're closed," he croaked. "How did you get in?"

"The door was open," Nolan said. "We came to see a Mr. Dalton."

"He's not here."

"Is he the owner?"

"I'm an owner," the man said. "Name's Tamerin, Mark Tamerin. Who're you?"

"I'm Detective Sergeant Andrew Sutton, Elizabeth Police. This is my partner, Detective Ed Nolan. Where is Mr. Dalton?"

"He's out on errands. What's this all about?"

"You say you're an owner. Are you Dalton's partner?" queried Sutton.

"Albert Dalton doesn't own any part of the business. He manages things. Runs the business. His wife, Geri, and I are partners in the bar business. I'm an accountant and keep track of finances, do the payroll, pay the taxes, pay the bills, apply for licenses, all that stuff. Al, he owns the building." Tamerin seemed a little more at ease knowing who the men were.

"Then let's you and us talk," said Nolan. "First put up that automatic under the newspaper. It's licensed?"

"I guess so. It's not mine, it's Dalton's"

"Ever shoot a gun?"

"No." Tamerin flushed at the stupidity of the way he handled things so far.

Sutton reached for the weapon, dropped the clip from the butt, ejected the chambered round and slipped it into his pocket. "I'll hold onto this for awhile, okay? What are you working on?"

"Last night's take. I count the money and make the deposits; pay the bills like I said."

"Why don't you put the cash drawer back?" Sutton's request was more an order than anything else.

Tamerin took the cash drawer to the register, inserted it, locked it up, returned to the card table, straightened out his piles of invoices and closed his check book. "What can I do for you?"

"We'd like to see the list of employees for the bar," commanded Sutton.

"I don't know what you're talking about."

"Are you a bar owner or not? The local Alcoholic Beverage Control Board wouldn't want to hear that. You're obliged to keep a list of your employees for inspection by any authority. Think hard."

"Oh, that list. I'll get it. It's hanging in the kitchen." Tamerin was now starting to perspire. He hustled into the kitchen, Nolan right behind him

"Here it is." He dodged Nolan and offered the sheets to Sutton.

"Is Ben Chusinsky on that list?"

"I never heard of him."

"He's supposed to be a manager here." Nolan's eyes bored into Tamerin.

"If he is, he never got paid. I don't recognize him on the payroll."

"You got a copy machine here someplace?" demanded Sutton.

"Yes. It's in the girl's dressing room."

"Make us a copy of these sheets, okay?"

Tamerin scurried into the dressing room with Nolan behind him. "I'll watch." Nolan grinned.

They returned to find Sutton poring over a stack of telephone bills. "You finished with these?" He stared at Tamerin.

"Be my guest."

"Mr. Tamerin," Sutton pocketed the bills and asked. "We'd like to take a look around, do you mind?"

"Not until you tell me what the hell this is all about."

"Seems Ben Chusinsky worked here up until the time he was murdered and dropped into the Arthur Kill," Sutton replied.

"Wait a minute. That's got nothing to with me or the bar."

"Maybe, maybe not but it would help us a lot if you would let us look around." Nolan appeared to take Tamerin into his confidence. "You would be a great help to us."

"Sure, go ahead. Anything I can do to help."

"We'll need a signed authorization from you allowing us to do so. Read this and sign it, please."

Tamerin looked over the preprinted form Sutton handed him. "This is pretty broad. I have no authority to allow you to look into the apartment upstairs. It's not part of the business. Neither is the small building in the back."

"Cross them out, initial the changes and sign it as owner and partner." Sutton was getting anxious. "And initial the part about not being threatened or promised anything to allow us to look around."

Tamerin hesitated.

"You don't have to let us, you know. We can always get a search warrant."

"I get the point," Tamerin answered and scribbled his name on the consent to search form.

"Thanks, Mark," Nolan said. "Maybe we should turn on the lights. That would also help."

Tamerin got up and went to the light panel. A few switches and the bar was ablaze with light.

"Show us around, would you?"

Tamerin guided them to the kitchen. The place was strewn with utensils, and food - wilted lettuce, shreds of sandwich meat, dried bread and a sink full of dirty dishes and dirtier, cold dish water. A refrigerator hummed in the corner. He reached under the sink and pushed down on the trap handle on Sutton's command. Only service knives and forks and spoons appeared.

"Board of Health been here lately?" Nolan asked.

"I wouldn't know. That's Dalton's area."

Sutton pulled open the utensil drawers. Nothing but greasy spoons, knives and forks. Sutton searched through the jumbled mass of metal. No signs of a murder weapon.

"Let's take a look in the dancer's dressing room."

Tamerin led them out of the kitchen toward the dressing room. The detective's eyes swept the bar area as they passed through. The rear wall was painted a flat black in sharp contrast to the soft beige walls throughout the rest of the room. The rear of the bar was also black from top to bottom and the floor was recently varnished.

"Eddy, take some polaroids of this area. I'll get Jerry Miner back with a search warrant." said Sutton.

"Who in their right mind would paint a mahogany bar black? Who would paint it anything? And the wall, black from floor to ceiling. Who's your interior decorator?" asked Nolan.

"Beats me," replied Tamerin casually. "That's also Dalton's area. I just keep the books."

The men had seen enough. They made a cursory inspection of the dressing room and walked around the bar twice, stopping at the front door.

"Tell Mr. Dalton to call me," Sutton said. "Here's my card. Tell him it's in his best interest. I want to see him at his earliest possible convenience."

Sutton and Nolan slumped in the front seat of the car. "There's only one reason to paint that area," mused Sutton.

"To cover blood stains," responded Nolan. "Beats trying to wash it down. Painting with a wide brush, they call it. Hell, even if we went back for blood splatters they would be of no value. They'd be covered or contaminated to the point of useless evidence."

"I think we're dealing with one shrewd ass-hole," Sutton growled. "Let's get back to the office."

"Did you give him back the automatic?"

"Screw him. Let him sue," Sutton growled. "I took it while you two were in the dressing room making copies; stuck a receipt for it in that pile of papers he was working on." Drew chuckled. "Wait 'til he finds it. He'll shit trying to make up some excuse for Dalton. We'll run it through ATF. Bet you a good cup of coffee it's stolen." Sutton paused.

"Accountant your ass," Sutton spat out. "He and Dalton's wife are on the license to keep the business from taking a rap for Dalton. That way if Dalton takes a hit, he still has income from the business or he can sell it."

Nolan jammed the car in gear and took off.

At headquarters Lt. Traxel listened to their oral report. "What now?"

Sutton pulled the telephone bills from his pocket. We have to make a database of these calls - sort by name, by number and by time and date."

"We don't have anybody here to do that," retorted Traxel.

"Larry Warner over at the Prosecutor's Office is in charge of the unit that handles that stuff," interjected Nolan, "I'll ask him."

"On the weekend?"

"Sure, he loves that stuff."

"And the search warrant?"

"It'll keep until Monday. We didn't see anything that would add to our affidavit," said Sutton. "And if it's forensics you're looking for; forget it. Dalton and company made sure of that. They painted the rear area black. All of it; floor to ceiling. He's been around the block a couple of times. The only thing that would have helped us is the knife and I didn't see anything that would have fit."

Traxel grabbed his coat. "See you Monday," he said. Turning, he growled, "And call Serfis. She called again this afternoon."

Chapter Five

8:00 pm - Friday, August 15th
The Apartment of Dr. Ariella Serfis

Drew Sutton stepped from the cab to the sidewalk, slammed the door, pushed a $10 bill through the open window and stuffed the change in his pocket. The address was scripted in gold leaf on the glass door - *"200 West End Avenue."* He checked his notebook. This is it? he mused. She didn't say anything about the building when I called. He craned his neck backwards to scan the forty one stories above him.

"Good evening, sir," the doorman crooned and held open the half inch thick glass entry door.

"Thanks."

A plush red carpet flecked with orange and blue led him over the terrazzo floored vestibule to the three steps of the raised concierge and elevator level. He nodded and strode by the concierge.

"May I help you, sir?" It was more a command than a request.

Drew walked over and sized him up; retired NYPD - it was written all over him. "Doctor Serfis," he responded.

"One moment please. I'll check to see if she's in. Your name, please?"

"Sutton. Andrew Sutton."

Detective Sutton surveyed the place. Nothing short of elegant. Clean, sparkling floor. Modest but beautifully designed chandelier. Sconces alternately held artificial candles and real ivy. Walnut panels. Is this guy carrying? Drew instinctively pressed his right elbow against the butt of his own Glock 9 mm automatic.

"The elevator bank to the left. Twenty first floor, sir. 21C."

No kidding, Drew muttered and noted the guardian did not record his name or time. The ride up was swift and smooth; Brahms enveloped the car. The door slid open and deposited him two doors to the left of 21C.

"Drew!! How nice of you to come," Ariella Serfis had been waiting, took his hand and tugged him into the apartment. Drew was stunned. She was wearing a pale orchid silk sheath with a flowing chiffon jacket. Pink toenails showed through the spaghetti strapped sandals.

"Doc," I'm sorry," he stammered. "I didn't know you were going out."

"Don't be silly. I'm not going out. I thought we'd have cocktails while we talked. Come in."

Drew felt as if he had stepped into the set of a 1940's romance film. The place reeked of money. A sunken living room opened to a glass wall facing west over the Hudson. A seven o'clock sunset glowed orange, pink, cerise, red at the horizon where dark gray clouds scudded across the scene. A small cocktail table was set up in front of a damask love seat. He turned to the dining room off to the left of what he supposed was the bedroom behind the living room.

"You like?" She looked him in the eye.

"Of course. It's just that I hadn't expected anything like this."

"Give me your jacket. Sit down." She pointed to the loveseat. "What will you have?"

"Well," Drew was fast getting used to the place. "How about a gin and tonic - slake the thirst, as they say."

"Gotcha. Turn on the stereo over there, will you, dear?"

Drew was getting that warm, uncomfortably comfortable feeling. Or was it warm and uncomfortable? Doctor Serfis had taken off her jacket revealing a fine upper torso. She walked in front of the glass wall and Drew admired the silhouetted legs under the silk sheath.

"Here you are. Let's drink to a final autopsy." She pulled a manila folder from the table behind them and gave it to Drew.

"What's in here that I need to know?" Drew didn't feel much like reading.

"I know the weapon."

"How?"

"After you left, George, the Deaner, was sewing up and found this in the spinal column." She handed him a small envelope. "It didn't show at x-ray."

Drew let slide the contents to the table. A piece of metal about ¾ of an inch long and a ¼ inch at its widest end fell out. It tapered off to a point. One edge appeared sharpened. "What the hell is it?"

"It's the point of a knife. If you were to extend the dimensions to the width of the wounds, I think I would say it was a boning knife." Ariella seemed pleased with the find.

"And what the hell is a boning knife?"

"It's a knife butchers use to trim the meat from bones. They are extremely sharp and, as you can see, thinner than the ordinary kitchen knife. I'd say this one had a blade of about six or seven inches."

"What are you saying; I should look for a butcher?"

"Not necessarily. Have you identified the body?"

"Yeah. Some low life outta Perth Amboy. Name's Chusinsky. Worked in a bar in Linden. A go-go place. We were there this afternoon."

"Have a kitchen?"

"Yeah. Some slop joint. Sandwiches and things. Nothing hot except some cooked shrimp. And some clams, too."

"Let me tell you something. When the boning knives get dull and won't hold an edge anymore, the butchers give them away to people who don't need so sharp an edge. Some people use them for opening clams."

Drew stared at her in amazement. "Where the hell did you learn that?"

"Drew," Ariella cautioned, "If you laugh at what I'm about to say; if you so much as snicker, chuckle or grin, I'll punch your lights out." She held her fist playfully against his chin.

Drew warmed at the touch. "Go ahead."

"My Father was a butcher."

The thought at the surgeon/pathologist being reared in a butcher shop was too much. He bit his cheek, he held his breath, and he clenched his teeth. Nothing worked. He looked at the impish grin on her face and burst into laughter. They laughed together and Ariella fell against him on the loveseat. It was but a moment and the laughter faded into a quiet, intimate meeting of the eyes. They pulled away and Drew cleared his throat.

"Well, that about does it." He rose.

"Oh, no you don't," she said, "Put that dammed cannon on the shelf in the entry closet. "I've made us a nice Caesar's salad. With clams."

"You're kidding!"

"Yes, I am. It's with shrimp." And she led him to the dining room.

The meal was pleasant but quiet. Walnut Queen Anne furniture. Lights adjustable to the occasion. A good Pinot Grigio and surprisingly homey, amiable company, "As Time Goes By" piped in from the living room stereo. They sat side by side at the six foot table.

"Why so quiet, Drew?"

"I don't know. Just a little overwhelmed, I guess."

"You, an ace detective, overwhelmed?"

"Yes, and I'm quick to admit it. Ari, we've worked together professionally for several years now. I can say I've looked at you in other ways. But I never in my wildest imaginings thought I'd be having a wonderful evening such as this. Never."

"It's nice, isn't it? And I have watched you more closely than you think. But you must be wondering about all this… this elegance. I'd be disappointed if you weren't."

"You want to tell me about it? I mean, from such…." Drew couldn't find the words.

"From such a modest family background?"

"Thanks."

"Take your wine glass. There's a balcony off the bedroom. We can sit there and talk and look out over the city."

The balcony was enclosed with grill work and airy with a breathtaking view of the city lights and sounds and the Hudson River. A sea-gull flew by shrieking. Drew saw it, furrowed his brow. On the twenty first floor? Trailing a piece of yellow ribbon? Tuxedo? The hair on his neck stood up. He wiped the gull from his thoughts.

"I'm ready," Drew said.

"The condo is mine. Worth about two and a half million. My half of the community property settlement from my divorce. He is a well known real estate broker and manager in the city who shall remain nameless. We just didn't have it after seven years. We had different views on about everything. We split and I changed my name back to my family name. I was thirty two at the time. That was four years ago. I'm thirty six if you've had too much wine," she grinned. "I'm able to keep it up with money my father left me. He was one of those hard working immigrants in Sheepshead. Never spent a dime unless he thought it over ten times. Always wanted to save so Mama would not be destitute when he died. As things turned out, she died first. That and my salary as a public servant keep me in the manner to which I became accustomed."

"Children?"

"Thankfully, no. Although we never really tried," Ari reflected. "How about yourself?"

"Well, never married. I've dated but never thought seriously about marriage. Never got along well with my Dad but Mom was swell. Was with the Office of Naval Intelligence for four years out of college. Got my B.A. in Political Science. Went back to school for six months and got a teaching certificate. Should have been an attorney. I'm thirty six, if you're counting. Been on the job ten years."

"Any regrets?" she asked.

"Not really. Like to do things right, be organized - one step at a time. That's what they say, anyway."

Ari got up and walked across to the bedroom door. She turned up the volume for the piped-in stereo and returned. The living room light caught the silhouette of her legs again. Drew moaned.

"Come, Drew. Dance with me a little."

Drew collapsed emotionally. He had tried to avoid the entanglement of a witness intimately consorting with another and failed. "Ari, Ari. Is this the right thing? I mean......

I mean. Don't get me wrong. I'm not a prude; but why me - us?"

She pulled his head down and whispered in his ear. "Because women like men who like women."

That did it. He was gone - emotionally trapped. All fear, all caution, all trepidation flew out the balcony door. "How would you like to play checkers?" he asked.

She pulled back her head and stared at him curiously. "What the hell does that mean?"

"One move and I'll jump you.'

She giggled and sagged against him. "Whatever you say, dear. Just be gentle with me."

Chapter Six

Sutton took the steps to the detective bureau two at time. He was late and he was happy. The weekend's love making with Ari lingered and he could smell her, feel her, taste her. And he could see her face framed in brunette on his pillow, her eyes alive with the pleasure of it all. He never had expected to stay the night let alone the weekend but had needed little coaxing.

He was jarred into reality when he tripped on the top step and lunged over the threshold into the bureau. The three secretaries stared, smiled and chorused a laugh.

"Shit," he muttered and strode into his cubicle.

He slipped out of his blazer and let it fall onto his chair, reading his telephone messages.

Penny Ancebia, one of the secretaries, slid in behind him and hung up his jacket. She looked around for prying eyes and put her hand on his butt and squeezed.

"What the hell are you doing?'

"Just getting a feel of things," she smiled.

Drew couldn't help it. He stared at her with a half-hidden smile in his eyes. "You're something and half," he said.

"When are you going to take me out?" she crooned.

"Never."

"Why not?"

Sutton tried to be as forthright as possible without hurting her feelings.

"Com'on Penny. Let's not play this game again. I like you. You're a good secretary and a great person to work with but if we go out, sex will rear its ugly head and we won't be friends anymore. Besides, you never dip your pen in the company inkwell."

Penny was a damn good secretary and a good source. She had unbelievable contacts on the street and he used them often -- small time hoods, girls on the street, nosey neighbors, all sorts and kinds of relatives, she knew them all. Yet she was squeaky clean herself. She could read his mind and flesh out reports without changing their meaning or jeopardizing a case. And she was head over heels in love with Drew Sutton.

"You've found someone else," she pouted.

"What does that mean? There was never a one to have an else for."

"Well, Drew, honey, when she tires of you, I'll be here."

Ed Nolan popped his head over the cubicle wall. Things were getting loud and he knew he had to break this up for everyone's sake. "Can we have a little quiet around here? I'm trying to get some sleep," he said playfully.

Penny hit him on the head with her steno pad. "By the way, there's a bimbo out in the interview room. Says she wants to talk to the detective on the Chusinsky case."

"What does she want?" Drew asked.

"Beats me. She didn't say," Penny strolled away with that cute little wiggle that had the entire detective division wondering what she was wearing under her dress.

Drew looked at Ed. "Tell Traxel I'll be in to the meeting shortly. I'll go talk to bimbo what's-her-name."

Nancy Horta was exactly what Sutton expected. What he didn't expect was her self-appointed guardian, Jose Marical, glaring at him. He was just about as ugly as guy could be – big, foreboding, with an ominous stare. Drew dismissed him with a sideward glance and told him to leave the room. "Police procedure," he said, "We think it best to talk to people alone so they won't be distracted." *Who needs you,* he thought, *to influence her statement. Take a hike.* Marical grumbled his retreat.

"Well, Miss Horta, how can I help you?" This was going to be interesting.

Lt. Traxel, Ed Nolan and Tommy Schneider, the Assistant Prosecutor assigned to the Elizabeth Police Department, were deep in conversation around the 6 foot oval table when Sutton walked into the conference room.

"Good morning," Schneider said.

"Well, well, the late Mr. Sutton." Traxel's voice was tinged with sarcasm.

"How did it go?" asked Nolan.

Good old Eddy, thought Drew. Always there with a timely change of subject. "Not bad. Not the most elegant of ladies but a source of information. She is the mother of Chusinsky's daughter and she came to apply for financial assistance through the Victim Witness program. Penny's typing up her statement now."

"What else?" asked Nolan.

"Name's Nancy Jean Horta, 32. Penny was right, a real bimbo. A paint job that would sink a battleship with hips the size of one. Ass-high red skirt and hooters hanging out of her blouse. She was introduced to Chusinsky by a mutual friend in Kansas City, Kansas and moved in with him. They banged around -- no pun intended -- Kansas, Illinois, Arizona, California, Florida.

Tennessee, Maryland. She's living in Pennsylvania now with a real wise guy; Colombian, gold up the ass, a pusher, mean looking bastard. I got his identifiers from her and gave them to narcotics on the way in.

"How did she find out about Chusinsky?"

"She says she hasn't received child support payments in about 8 months and came in to inquire. They told her in Essex County."

"Essex County? Bullshit." Said Traxel

"Probably the local grapevine. Maybe Dalton." said Schneider.

"She says Chusinsky used pills mainly, Quaaludes, pain killers."continued Sutton. "Finally found a doctor in Middletown who would write scrip and became a small time pusher. She and Chusinsky were on and off and he got a job in Washington, D.C. managing parking garages for some national outfit and started living in Maryland. She took the baby and left him when he beat her up one night. Hasn't seen him in two years."

"How old is the baby?" asked Schneider. "What were they doing in Essex County?"

"Five. Grimmer -- that was her maiden name -- applied for child support in Essex County when his job brought him back to New Jersey. She had the order forwarded to Kansas City. She subsequently moved to Phoenix and met Marical.

Some people will do anything for a constant source and a gorilla's protection."

"So?" asked Traxel.

"So, we know what he was into; who the woman is in the child support order Ed found in Essex County the other day. I'll give you her statement when it's typed."

Drew eyed the stack of dot matrix printouts in front of Traxel. "What's that?"

Nolan pushed them to Drew. "Those are the database printouts of the telephone numbers Larry Warner compiled."

Drew whistled and flipped through the stack. "Cripes; the pile is two inches thick."

"There are three sets: one sorted by telephone numbers called, one in date and time order of calls made, and one with the most frequent numbers called. We don't have names and addresses yet," explained Nolan.

"I called telephone security. They will fill them in for us," said Traxel.

"Without a court order?"

"Don't need one yet. But it's coming down to that soon," said Schneider. "Get these over to the security office ASAP."

"That was one of the smarter things you've done lately. Anything else?" said Traxel.

"Oh, shit. I almost forgot. We know what the murder weapon was," grinned Drew and handed the autopsy report to Traxel.

"When did you get this?"

"Friday night."

"What do you mean, Friday night?" glowered Traxel.

"Remember you told me Dr. Serfis called? Well, I went over and picked up the report. She said the knife used was a thin stiletto type blade, very pointy and widening to about ¾ of an inch. This one was about seven inches long, probably a boning knife like the ones butchers use."

Traxel peered into the envelope containing the knife point and scanned the autopsy protocol and death certificate. "Enter these things into evidence and report to me in my office – and don't make any stops along the way." Traxel jumped up and left leaving Sutton, Nolan and Schneider in sudden silence.

"I don't want to hear this," said Schneider, leaving.

Nolan looked at Drew in consternation. "I'm partnered with a lover and a dumb one at that."

"What do you mean?"

"Jesus Christ, Drew. Traxel's been around. What in hell is the matter with you? You have a great knack for jamming yourself up. You could have said Friday afternoon and let it go at that." He shook his head and left. "Your brains are in your pecker," he said.

Drew leaned back and heaved a sigh. Lets' get to it, he thought and grabbed the knife point and autopsy report and headed for the evidence vault.

Lieutenant Traxel always demanded to know the current status of every case in the detective bureau. He hated surprises, despised secrets and Sutton's clandestine visit to Doctor Serfis was both a surprise and a secret. He was never one to mince words – he told it as he saw it and was right 99 percent of the time. He was sure of himself now. He loomed over Sutton in his chair.

"What's your relationship with Doctor Serfis?"

"Strictly professional."

"Professional how?"

"Just professional; she's the pathologist and I'm the lead investigator on the case," Drew showed no emotion.

"Let's get this straight, Sergeant," Traxel hissed. "If your relationship is other than professional, you've violated one of the cardinal rules of court and this department and you'll hear about it. You'll lose time, maybe your stripes, maybe your job. Don't break another. The next time you see her make sure it's on a strictly professional level – my definition, not yours. And on company time only. Kabish?"

"Yes, sir."

"Drew, I've got some bad vibes on this. Keep your fly zipped." Traxel stared at him. "Well?"

"Well, what."

"Go pick up those subscriber names and addresses," growled the Lieutenant.

Eddy Nolan didn't look up when Drew dragged himself into the conference room. It had taken him an entire day to sort out the names and addresses of each subscriber and assign them the proper telephone numbers in the databases. Now he was counting, trying to determine whatever pattern there might be, mulling over potential witnesses and their interviews.

"You'll love this," he raised his head and pointed to the stacks. "This will take two weeks on the streets."

"Morning, Eddy," Drew was sleepy eyed.

Nolan looked up at him warily. "You paying any attention at all to what the boss said?"

Sutton didn't respond. Nolan shook his head slowly and returned to his papers. "One hundred and ninety number assignments. Some obviously vendors. Some business types. Others need looking into. Over 800 calls all told."

Sutton woke up, sat down opposite Nolan and pulled the pile to himself. "How about the night of his disappearance?"

"This will annoy you. Maybe even interest you." Nolan couldn't resist the sarcasm. There are three days of no calls made from that phone starting the day after Mr. Chusinsky drove his son to work."

Sutton looked across the table at Nolan; the sarcasm hadn't escaped him and the pleasure of the last three nights with Ari turned to an icy lump in his throat. "Two things, Eddy. First, lay off the smart-ass remarks. We've been friends for a long time. Let's keep it that way, okay?

"Sorry."

"Second, this is a fantastic job you and Warner have done and I'm sure Traxel appreciates it. I do and Mrs. Chusinsky will, too. You may have fixed the crime date. That is a public phone. How did Dalton keep people from using it?"

"Beats me. Probably hung an out-of-order sign on it."

"When did the calls start up again?'

"Don't know. The bill date ends the date of the last blank day."

"In other words the three days of no activity end on the last billing date."

Nolan nodded. "The next bill won't be out for another two weeks. The phone is still listed as a working number in the telephone company files."

"How about the phone in his apartment?"

"Beat you to it. Got a subpoena for it. Records show it was temporarily disconnected at the customers' request the day after the calls stopped being made from the public phone."

"And before that?"

"Hardly any - a handful."

Nolan and Sutton stared at each other trying to pry the significance from each other.

Sutton heaved himself from his chair. "This will take awhile. Let's separate the names into three piles. One high priority - where several calls were made to a particular individual. Another for fewer calls to particular people and the last for obvious business calls - vendors and the like. Then let's divvy them up and compare notes after each day."

"We're going to need some help on this," Nolan said. "We're looking at two weeks work."

"Ask Traxel for some help."

Nolan got up and went for the door. "By the way, Mrs. Chusinsky called. Wanted to know how we're making out."

"And?"

"Told her we're making progress."

Sutton ached for the woman. *It's a fib but it will keep her hopes alive and her from calling for awhile.*

Nolan returned. "Traxel gave us Tommie Milnar and the Prosecutor's Office is sending Norm Kaspar."

The two detectives pored over the lists. Their feet ached in anticipation of the next couple of weeks or so on the street.

Chapter Seven

10:00 am – Wednesday, September 3rd
Office of the Prosecutor

Assistant Union County Prosecutor Tommy Sedgewick pushed the rimless glasses to his forehead and massaged the strain from his eyes, flipped closed the cover of the 2 1/2" thick file and pushed it to the center of his desk. He swiveled his chair, tilted back, put his feet up on the back work table, clasped his hands behind his balding head and smiled at the warmth of the morning sun that drenched his face and chest through the window.

Sedgewick was a career Assistant Prosecutor and had supervised the Homicide Unit for the last ten of his 23 years on the job. Two more years and he was out - retired - and would take with him an admirable record of successful prosecutions. Now he mulled over his latest, *State v. Dalton*. The file was partitioned typically into four sections: police reports, evidence list, witness list and witness statements. He had read the police reports, scanned the scanty evidence list and pored over the witness list telling him what the witnesses might testify to. The 1" stack of statements he had riffled in contemplation and set aside. *Not one bit of irrefutable evidence. All circumstantial, speculation and theory*, he mused. *Good god, this is State v. whom?*

Sutton's rap on his open door jarred him from his contemplation and he repositioned his glasses.

"Drew, Eddy, come on in. Thanks for coming over." He rose from his chair to shake hands.

"Morning," Drew responded. He draped his coat on the coat rack, closed the office door and dropped into a chair facing Sedgewick across his desk. Eddy Nolan pulled a chair from the corner and slid into it next to Sutton.

"I need some help on this Dalton matter, fellas. I've read your investigative reports and patrol's initial reports and they pretty well outline the case. But evidence is scanty: nothing more than an autopsy protocol and the pointed end of the murder weapon, the plastic sheet he was wrapped in, the flowery bedspread, the electrical cord and the duct tape. Nothing else - no prints, no weapon, no blood, no forensics of any evidentiary value. There are a lot of statements but no eye witnesses. I haven't read all the statements. Thought maybe you could give me your reactions to these people - what they're saying and what they may know as compared to what they said." Sedgewick pushed the file to the two detectives.

Drew exhaled a tired sigh. Ignoring the file he pushed it to Eddy. "This case starts with a wrapped up, naked body in the water - how long? A week; ten days?"

Sedgewick sensed the testiness, the defensiveness in his tone. "Drew let's start off on the right foot, okay?" He glanced at Eddy. "Nothing that will be said here cannot and should not be considered critical of the investigation. This is a real whodunit and I appreciate any frustrations you might have. So let's start by telling me about the evidence. We *are* looking for an indictment; are we not?"

Drew took a slow breath and relaxed. "Okay. First off, I measured the outdoor electrical extension cord. It appears to have been a 50 footer with 12 feet cut out of the middle. These things come in 25, 50 and 100 feet lengths and can be bought in any hardware store or most supermarkets. I don't know why anyone would want to use something like that to tie up a body but they did. Eddy tried, but it can't be traced. The pieces measured 38 feet total. I think it was a 50 footer.

"You did a warrantless search of the premises, I see. Any sign of the missing piece?"

"We did a consensual search of the Go-Go premises. Nothing. But we went back with a warrant later and searched the entire premises and property including the apartment above. Again, nothing."

"What about the bedspread?"

"No help. It's a twin bed size spread. Thought we might find its mate in the apartment. Nothing."

"Anything else?"

Eddy joined in. "I sent the duct tape to the FBI lab hoping to find some prints on the tape. The report came back negative. I can't believe a guy could not leave prints on at least the sticky side. But that's what the report said." He shrugged his shoulders and slouched back in his chair.

"Can we place the victim at the scene; that's assuming that was the scene? Any forensics - any blood, maybe?"

"During the period between the murder and the discovery of the body, the cook, Bobby Lerker, painted the rear of the bar area, including the bar, with black paint. If there was any blood spattering, it was painted over. We used a UV light. No body fluids showed; including the ceiling." Drew sighed in resignation and sagged.

"What makes you think the murder took place at the rear of the bar? What makes you think it took place anywhere on those premises?"

"It's the last place anyone we talked to can place him. And besides; why the hell would somebody paint it if not to cover something up? Especially during the period we're talking about?"

"What did Lerker say?"

"Can't find him. He lives in the city somewhere. Intelligence at NYPD makes him a Westie - you know, the Irish mafia on the west side. Dalton said he doesn't know where Lerker is. He said he was upset that Lerker skipped leaving him without a cook. Dalton said he told Lerker to paint it to give the area mystique, an intimate, mysterious atmosphere. Bullshit." Sutton was getting agitated and rose in his chair.

Eddy glanced at Drew and took the conversation away from him. "There are only two people who knew what happened and where. One's dead. The other ain't talking."

"And there are no eye witnesses?"

"None that we know of," Drew retorted.

Sedgewick swiveled 90 degrees to his right and stared at the wall. He tugged his lower lip and spun back. "Christ, Drew. You're not giving me much to work on. How about these statements. Anybody saying anything helpful?"

"Not really. All we can put together is Dalton had the ability and the propensity for violence. He beat up a couple of guys at his old place in Hazlet. Threatened some wise guy with a knife. But nobody's talking. I've never seen so many people afraid to talk."

"Yes," Eddy chimed in, "We get cases where one or two get all kinds of nervous on questioning so we know where to concentrate. But this - this is ridiculous. Everbody's nervous, nobody's talking"

"How about Dalton. What's he got to say for himself?"

"This guy is as slippery as a bar of soap in the bathtub. He knew Chusinsky. Let him do a couple of odd jobs - schedule the girls; bartend some. Gave him a place to crash in the apartment above the bar. Paid him in cash; what else, right? But other than that he won't admit to anything," said Eddy.

"Says the last time he saw him was on a Sunday morning about August 3rd when Chusinsky got a phone call from somebody and had to leave fast. Something about owing a guy two grand. Dalton lent it to him. Hasn't seen him since," added Sutton.

"Anybody with him at the time?"

"He says no; but who knows," responded Sutton.

"Anybody else of interest," asked Sedgewick

They went over the statements - the dancers who knew nothing but liked Chusinsky. The customers - who knew nothing but liked Chusinsky.

They stopped at the statement of Margarita Garcia.

"Now here is someone with knowledge but freezes when the name Dalton jumps up," Sutton growled. "She is one of the girls who parked in front of Chusinsky's place and Mrs. Chusinsky took down the plate. She comes from Queens and is a steady - or was a steady - dancer at the Haunt. Says she spent a night with him every now and then but hasn't seen him in months. Can't remember the last time."

"She freezes?"

"She is scared shitless. Nervous as hell. Trembles and fidgets at the idea we think she may know something. Her eyes dart and move about - won't look you straight in the face. Talks about her relationship with Chusinsky but gets lockjaw when we get to the last time she saw him or any dealings with Dalton. She knows what happened but absolutely refuses to say anything about any homicide."

"Maybe an hour in front of the Grand Jury will loosen her up."

"Maybe. If you can find her. Haven't seen or heard from or about her since we talked to her. Her mother gives us the "no comprende" shit when we call," griped Sutton.

Sedgewick leaned back, hands clasped behind his head. He closed his eyes and tried to make sense of this incomprehensible situation. "Let's move on," he directed. "Who is Billy Maledict?"

Sutton drew a breath. "He's a local scummer out of Staten Island. Now lives in Hazlet with his latest squeeze, Molly O'Brien, and her ten year old boy. We're looking at him because of the many phone calls to his house in Staten Island and O'Brien's house. About 5 of the 15 phone calls to her house came on the morning of August 3rd. She says Maledict answered the phone and took the calls in the living room. She heard him call his brother Roger who came around with his van and they drove off together."

"What time was that?"

"About 5 o'clock Sunday morning."

"What is his background?"

"He pushes some crack, marijuana, pills. Sells used cars that he buys in Pennsylvania at auction. She thinks he steals certificates from the DMV office in Rahway."

"Probably steals the cars, too," interjected Nolan.

"His brother just got out of Attica for blowing away some neighbor's dog with a shotgun in an apartment building. His father did time for murder 20 years ago."

"Maybe you're looking at the wrong guy. Maybe Maledict is the killer," mused Sedgewick. "He sure has all the credentials and maybe we can tie him into the scene. Will Molly testify in front of a Grand Jury?"

"Are you kidding? He'd kill her and she knows it. He's beat her up a couple of times already. Besides, I told her she wouldn't have to. I'd rather go back on my word when I need to. If I turn her around now, she'll never trust me when I really need her."

"How did Maledict react to your questions?"

"He was kind of hinky. Talked fast, you know that nervous fast talk with all the giggles in between. Came up with the usual disclaimer, 'As God is my witness, I don't know nothin' about what you're talkin.' or 'I swear on my Mothers' grave', the same old bullshit. One thing though, when I showed him the picture of the bedspread, he winced. Ever so slightly but he winced. I think he knows the whole story."

"Sounds like a good candidate for the Grand Jury," mulled Sedgewick.

"There's one problem," retorted Nolan. "He's unreliable as a witness. His record stinks; he's a liar and sounds and acts like one. Without corroboration he has no testimonial value. If you ever went to trial, they'd tear him apart on the stand."

Silence hung in the air as the three regrouped emotionally.

"Do we know the direction from which the body came?" Sedgewick broke the silence.

"Not really," muttered Nolan. "Went to the Coast Guard on that one. The Kill is a tidal river. It connects to the Raritan Bay at one end and Newark Bay at the other. The tide rises and ebbs about two and half hours apart from each end causing the current in the Kill to reverse direction according to the tides. Because we don't know when the body was dumped, the body could have come from the north or the south. It could have floated back and forth for a week or whatever time it was in the water."

"Jake Harney was willing to bet it came from the south," chuckled Sutton. "I can just see you now trying to get the judge to accept him as an expert witness."

"And Harney is probably right," retorted Sedgewick.

The three sank into their thoughts trying to salvage some sense from the conversation; some direction; some impetus to push this thing off top dead center.

The phone jarred them into reality. Sedgewick picked it up.

"It's for you," he held it out to Sutton. "Lt. Traxel."

It was a Hollywood type conversation - one sided and curious to Sedgewick and Nolan. "Yes Lieu.....What?...... How do we know that?....... Where is he now?.........Oh shit."

"Dalton split," Sutton explained and hung up. "Sold the business and the property to a developer. Happened Friday. They think he's in Florida   Everything was handled by his attorney who acted as power of attorney and he's not talking - some sort of confidentiality crap. A guy on the liquor license board saw an envelope with a Florida postmark but no return address. They've already prepared a plot plan for demolition and rebuilding for submission to the building inspector. There goes the crime scene and any evidence in it. We're up the creek."

"Christ," Nolan said, "It's only been a month since the homicide. How could he find a buyer in that short a time?"

"It's a Go-Go bar. He probably had a buyer lined up from before," noted Sedgwick, "These bars move pretty fast, especially if you want out in a hurry."

"And if it's only the real estate that has been sold, the liquor license can be held in abeyance by the technical owners, his wife and Tamerin," added Sutton.

"We'd better be up to Traxel's office," said Nolan. "I'm sure he's going to have his own thoughts on this.

///

Lt. Traxel studied his two detectives from behind his desk. "That's it?" he asked. "No evidence, no witnesses? No case either."

"But we can't just let him skate," moped Nolan.

"No justice for Mrs. Chusinsky," said Sutton.

"Fellas," announced Traxel, "I've got a detective bureau to run. Cases are starting to pile up. I'm putting this on the back burner. You're both back in rotation. If something comes up, let me know."

Traxel grabbed a pile of papers and sorted through them. Nolan and Sutton were dismissed.

Silently they dragged themselves to the parking lot and stopped between their cars. Sutton stuffed his hands in his pockets. Nolan leaned back against his car craning his neck and head upwards. They looked at the ground, searched the sky, glanced at each other. The let down was sudden and hard.

"I've got some time coming," mused Sutton. "Friday is my last day before a two week vacation," he said. "I'll put in for it tomorrow. I need to clear out the cobwebs. Maybe I'll come up with something."

"Sure," answered Nolan. "Keep in touch. I'm taking the next two days myself."

They drove off.

Chapter Eight

10:00 am – Thursday, September 4th
18 Loomis St., Elizabeth, NJ

Sutton sat in the rocker in his basement apartment. It was cozy enough and the boiler that had been walled off from the rest of the basement kept him more than warm. Eddy's widowed aunt, Kathleen DeHaven, offered him the vacancy when he left his father's apartment. He leaned back, three fingers of Scotch in one hand the other gripped around the arm of the rocker. He mulled over the things that brought him to a point in his life he would never have imagined.

His birth certificate read Andrew Daniel Sutton – Place of Birth: Elizabeth General Hospital; Date of Birth: July 17, 1957 – the Sutton's lived on Magnolia Avenue off 5th Street.

Drew's mother, Heidi, was a German girl his father, Daniel, met while on occupation in West Berlin in 1947. It didn't take long for the handsome American G.I. to fall for the pretty girl who was alone and hungry after being orphaned during the bombing of Dresden. She lived with her two older cousins who had their own problems and gave her little time. But she was clean, neat in her dress and habits and avoided the temptations of the streets. She was loyal and faithful and the twenty-year-old showed a steadfastness Daniel admired. They fell in love and married.

Daniel brought her to the States in 1949. It soon became apparent he was more infatuated than in love. Faced with the arrival of Andrew and all the responsibilities it brought, he became emotionally hollow. He was an independent sort – something that kept him from gaining his Army Sergeant's stripes – and soon regretted the marriage. He spent hours at the local bars carousing with the gang. By the time Andrew was 6, Heidi had become the target of drunken and verbal abuse.

Andrew took it all in and sympathized with his mother. In turn, Heidi poured all her affection on the son who adored her. He ran errands, helped with chores, sang songs with her and sat with her at night reading, doing his homework, listening to her stories and learning the German language.

Heidi, meanwhile, found a friend in Maggie Nolan, a widowed neighbor, 3 doors down. They shared their loneliness, went to Bingo, took their sons to mass on Sundays and became the family each had been robbed of. Eddy, Maggie's only child, and Drew – a year younger – became as brothers. They went to grammar school together, played on Saint Patrick's High School basketball team and served as altar boys at church.

When Drew was 15, the Sutton family's problems were magnified by Heidi's untimely death – caused by a venereal infection she was able to avoid in her war-torn country yet given to her by a carousing husband. She died heartbroken. Through bitter tears Drew, helped by the Nolans, attended to the arrangements and buried his mother with the support of a few friends. It would be the last time he would cry. His father, in a continual drunk, did not attend.

Drew paused in his reverie and sipped from his glass of Dewars and thought about his decision to leave his father. He had known then they would have it out sooner than later and to avoid a certain confrontation, Drew packed up and moved to a spare basement apartment in the house Eddy's Aunt Kathleen owned on Loomis Street - far enough away from his father and close enough to Eddy's house and Saint Patrick's High.

Eddy Nolan had graduated a year ahead of Drew and joined the Elizabeth Police force with a good word from Father Pagano, Police Chaplain and Pastor at Saint Patrick's church. He pulled the 3 to 11 shift and the boys saw less of each other although Eddy always had an eye and an ear open for Drew's well being. But Drew was unhappy and listless. He yearned for the direction, order and guidance of his mother. He buried himself in his studies and got above average grades. Father Pagano convinced his friend, U.S. Representative Tony Shires, to recommend Drew for the Naval Academy where he graduated an Ensign in 1979 and was assigned to the Office of Naval Intelligence. His mother's teaching of German and attention to detail earned him a promotion to Lieutenant Junior Grade while serving - not coincidentally - as a junior intelligence officer at the American Embassy in West Berlin. But the possibility of years of desk duty gnawed at him and rather than risk it, he fulfilled his service obligation, resigned his commission and hopped a military flight to Elizabeth to kick back and figure out his next move.

Drew rocked and smiled. *Good old Eddy*, he mused. It hadn't taken Eddy long to convince him to join the Elizabeth Police force. The irony of course, was he wound up a Sergeant ahead of Eddy because of some good test scores, a good education and a veteran's preference. He had learned the art of intelligence analysis and was good at applying it to the job. Eddy had 5 years more time and had developed an uncanny sense of street smarts. But they were equals on the job and both knew it.

None of which helped. With Traxel's decision to shelve the investigation, it would be back to the old grind of assaults, burglaries, strong arm robberies and whatever else came down the pike. Shit. He felt good about taking the time off.

Chapter Nine

Noon - September 10th
Grand Hyatt Hotel, New York City

The phone call had caught Sutton coming out of the shower.

"I'm calling for Mike." the man said. "He needs... he has to see you. Noon. Restaurant. Grand Hyatt, Forty Second St. Saturday. Got it?"

Sutton blubbered through the towel on his face. "Say again?"

The voice repeated the instructions and hung up. *This guy is either a nut or he has something on the Chusinsky homicide. But why the mystery? Why the hocus pocus? And how did he get my number?*

Detectives are an innately curious bunch, especially if it involves them personally, and this spooked him.

Sutton stood under the marquee of the Grand Hyatt Hotel with his back against the wall. He surveyed the sea of bobbing heads passing him on 42nd Street not knowing what to look for or who to look for. No one looked at him; everybody ignored him. He saw no one he recognized or, he thought, no one who could have been interested in him. *What the hell,*

he mumbled; *the guy told me 12 noon in the restaurant of the Grand Hyatt. It's 11:55. Let's do it.* He shuffled through the slowly revolving glass door and took the twelve steps up to the main level. He strode past the registration desk across the expansive lobby and climbed the five steps to the restaurant level.

"One for lunch?" the maitre d' asked.

"It'll be two," Sutton responded. "I'm expecting another person - unless he's here already."

"Mr. Sutton?"

Drew eyed the man suspiciously, "Yes."

"Your party may be delayed. Use this entry card for the rest room." He pushed the card into Sutton's hand. Sutton felt paper underneath.

The Maitre d' busied himself at his podium. Sutton stared at him.

The headwaiter didn't look up. "You might want to use it now," he murmured through his teeth placing a subtle emphasis on the last word.

Sutton took the hint and followed the signs to the men's room. The paper was a square reception announcement type envelope. He tore it open. Room 310 was written on the paper enclosed. That's it? Room 310? Sutton had been agitated but now he was pissed. He headed to the exit. *The hell with this bullshit. I'm out of here.* He took three steps and braked to a stop, looking blankly at the floor, the note still in his hand. He was still a cop; still curious. He stuffed the envelope in his pocket and turned to the bank of elevators.

The 3rd floor was a long five foot wide hallway. The room doorways were recessed, illuminated by the hall ceiling lights and a light on either side of the alcove. He found 310, looked up and down the hall and rapped on the door. He heard the scritch of the peephole cover and backed out of the alcove into the hall. Leaning his left shoulder against the wall, his free right hand on the butt of his off-duty Walther .38 PPK Special, he peeked into the alcove. The door cracked open, the safety chain still in place.

"Sutton?" the voice asked.

"Yeah."

The door closed and the safety chain rattled loose.

Sutton pulled his PPK and leaped through the door pushing the man backwards onto the nearest bed.

He stood at the foot of the bed and held the PPK on Mike Hagerty.

"Don't move," he screamed. "What the hell is going on here?" Cat-like, Sutton flung open the bathroom door, looked around and satisfied himself no one was behind the shower curtain. He pulled back the closet doors. No one there.

He quickly scanned the room. A typical business room - round table for four; two double beds, chest of drawers with a Philips TV in the cabinet on top and a writing table.

Hagerty was trying to scramble from the bed where he had landed. "Goddammit, Sutton, what the hell is this tough guy shit, anyway?"

Sutton was panting. "Sit down and shut up. Listen to me you fucking idiot. How am I supposed to know who's in here? With all this chicanery and skullduggery you had me to the point of blowing your brains out. You understand? You could have been dead on the floor and me in handcuffs."

They sat at the table eyeing each other.

Sutton broke the silence. "Want to tell me what this all about?"

Hagerty stared back. Breathing seemed hard for him.

Sutton was dismayed at the sight of him. He was not the correct, uniformed, imposing figure Sutton was used to saluting on his way to Ari's apartment. He appeared slight, weary, resigned and unsettled. Sutton wanted to apologize for his outburst.

"Name's Mike Hagerty. Retired NYPD."

"I figured that out a long time ago."

"Can I call you Drew?"

"Go ahead, Mike."

Hagerty leaned back. Sutton bent forward with his forearms on the table. Hagerty was quickly thoughtful, appraising Sutton, measuring the man. Sutton bored into Hagerty, analyzing and assessing his motives and actions.

"Drew, I've checked you out. One of the good guys; a good cop - does the right thing.

"Get to it, Mike. Forget the intro; I'm also modest and blush easily."

"Drew, get serious; this is as important to you as it is to me. You're a brother officer. I spent seven years in Internal Affairs. I know a bum when I see one. I watch when you and Dr. Serfis leave and come back. She's your main squeeze, ain't she?"

Sutton bristled at the term and glowered at Hagerty.

"Oh, shit," said Hagerty, "It's for real isn't it?"

Sutton went deep within himself. Twice he had told her not to tell him she loved him. Often they spoke of the temporary nature of things. Yet often he felt the helplessness at the touch of her hand on his arm, the light hearted banter, the serious conversation. "I suppose so." It was an admission he had yet to make until now. "How did you get my number?"

"Private Eye. He owed me a couple. He's the guy who called."

"It must have cost you a couple of bucks. Guess it is important."

"I said he owed me."

"And the head waiter? The room?"

"C'mon, Drew. How long have you been on the job?"

Things were quieting down. They spoke with more respect, their estimation of each other rose.

"Hagerty, if you don't tell me what's going on I'm going to reach across the table and choke you like a chicken," he said with a half laugh.

"You're being tailed."

Sutton's jaw drooped. *How he could have missed it? Who? What for?*

"The Feds - the Bureau and DEA. They took the apartment next to Dr. Serfis. Her place is wired. Might even be scoped. You're on tape, maybe in pictures."

"In the bedroom?"

"I don't know."

"C'mon; this is bullshit. How do you know.? Are you certain? "

"It's the truth. Went to the FBI Academy with one of the narcs. We got to be good friends. I gave him a couple of good cases. He's seen me there and knows what I do. He asked me to keep an eye out."

"Why? What the hell has Ari, er, Dr. Serfis got to do with anything?"

"He told me they're working a money laundering case. Seems a couple of shitheads are trustees in some sort of foundation. They're supposed to give grant money to outfits in South America for helping kids get good medical care, education and that crap. What really happens is that the South American charities are fronts for the drug cartels and they make applications for grants and, of course, the American foundation ships them the money. The money is really drug money from the proceeds of operations up here. The money comes in from the two trustees, Andre Salinas, a councilman from Brooklyn and a Hector Lopez, another councilman from Harlem, the Bronx. They're real heavy hitters."

"And how does that involve Dr. Serfis?"

"She's the Director of the Foundation - Americans for Children Foundation."

Sutton's head fell into his hands. He could barely breathe. "Is she in on this?"

"I don't know. The Feds seem to think so but they're not sure. Most of what they got so far is some sweet music, clinking glasses," Hagerty winked, "and your phone calls."

"And some heavy breathing," Sutton groaned. He leaned back in his chair and looked up at the ceiling. His mind raced backwards. Back to all the autopsies. Back to Ari's apartment. Back to her willing and sincere love. He reviewed his calls. What did he say? What did she say? Back to the department and what future might be left for him there. Sutton moaned, "Oh, shit."

Hagerty read his mind. "They're gonna rip you apart. You'll be pounding a beat or filing traffic reports - if you have a job left."

"Why are you telling me this? You're passing confidential info. You're risking your pension. If anybody finds out, you're gone. You won't even be able to sling hamburgers, nobody'll want to be seen with you."

"Don't mean diddley to me," Hagerty shrugged. "I'm a dead man anyway."

"How's that?"

"You haven't asked me if I've told Dr. Serfis. You never asked me how I feel or how anybody feels about her. I've waved you through every time you come into the building. no sign in; no nothing," Hagerty ran on, his words tumbling out.

He paused to gather his wits. "Me and my family, we're grateful to Dr. Serfis. I will probably die in eight months. I was diagnosed with leukemia about six months ago. They gave me four months and I started getting ready. I stopped feeling sorry for myself and spoke to Dr. Serfis. Who should know better than a pathologist, right? Well, she took me and my wife and gave us a good talking to; pointed me in the right direction. Pumped up my wife."

"She's got me hooked up with some experimental treatment in Canada. Who knows? It may work. And even if it don't, Dr. Serfis gave me about eight months - maybe a year I didn't have before. She's a great lady. I don't care what they find out." His words were coated with affection

Sutton looked at Hagerty with anguish. He wished he could take back the roughing up he gave him. "Will you tell Ari?"

"Oh no. That's your job. I don't want anything happening to her. I just hope I'm helping."

"And if she's involved?"

"Who knows and I don't care. She's can't know I know. Get it?" His voice rose. "This never came from me."

Drew nodded.

"Sutton, you and I are finished for now. I won't see you again except to wave you through. Okay?"

"Yes, sir." The "sir" was spontaneous and emphasized with uncontrolled warmth. "And if ever you need anything from me, if there's anything I can do for you….," he paused.

What a ridiculous thing to say. Here's a guy about to die and I'm offering him nothing, really. "or your family, you have my number."

They shook hands and Drew left. He never saw the tears in Hagerty's eyes.

///

Sutton hung his head over his steaming morning cup of coffee. He let the vapors into his sinuses and the caffeine into his bloodstream to fight a glorious hangover. It was a losing battle. Last night's bout with John Barleycorn ended as usual - Drew lost and nature was now cashing in her chips.

He wanted to think, needed to think, sort things out, get a grip on what was happening and couldn't. Just getting up had drained him, sapped him of effort and worse, sapped him of his will to think. He fumbled for the refrigerator door, took out the V-8 and poured himself a glass - no vodka. On the way back to bed he made a pit stop hoping he wouldn't flush his brains down the toilet.

It was 1:00 o'clock in the afternoon when his gnawing stomach woke him and Sutton tried the coffee again. This time he made it. Two scrambled eggs, some pre-cooked bacon and two slices of rye toast and he felt human. Maybe he could sort things out. He wandered around the kitchen, did the dishes and took out a pad and pencil and doodled. It helped when he doodled and he needed all the help he could get thinking about yesterday's events. He had disconnected the phone. The last thing he needed now was a call from Ari.

Was she in on this? Their phone calls were innocuous; never any mention of anything except their dates and a hint of their love life. The Feds could pick up nothing from their calls. Maybe they got information from her other calls to who knows who; but never from theirs. But that didn't prove anything. Yet she mentioned her trust early on but never anything about the foundation. Why? And besides, when did she ever become involved with a foundation dealing with South American kids? Did her autopsies ever involve drug dealers? If so, what benefit could she derive without blowing her cover? The thoughts sped through his mind.

How did he ever become involved? Where did he make the wrong turn? If she was involved, why and how did he miss it? He was a detective; a cerebral one he was once told. He surely would have detected something - some slip of the tongue, some mysterious act on her part. She never asked him anything about police work; she would have, wouldn't she? And besides; who gives a shit? He could simply walk away, right?

The last question jarred loose the remaining sleep from his brain. By now the Feds would have contacted his chief. He would not have known, he was on vacation and sick leave and no one would have told him. Of course! Eddy Nolan hadn't called him in a couple of weeks; something he usually does. Drew was so busy with Ari he hadn't noticed the time passing by. *They knew! The bosses knew! He'd be suspended the minute he showed up; maybe fired or worse yet, arrested. All because some goddam shit head, some friggin' scumbag was killed over a couple of grand and Drew had taken Jackie Ryan's call.*

Sutton relived the events, the discovery of the body, the autopsy, his meetings with Ari, the dead end leads, the eventual cold case syndrome and Mrs. Chusinsky. *Yes, Mrs. Chusinsky.* He could still see her: the short little housewife and mother.

The chubby face. Her neat and simple clothes. Her plain face; its only makeup was pain, honesty and devotion. Her pleading eyes - *won't you please do something? Who killed my boy?*

Sutton had been a devoted son. He had loved his mother and her reward was a bright and lawful, well mannered young man who loved and respected all mothers. And now he pitied Mrs. Chusinsky. Her reward was a body wrapped in plastic - a floater in the Kill. He had to find some reward, some sense of justice for her.

Enough vacation. Enough honey this and darling that. Love is supposed to add something to your life not take away. He couldn't call Ari at home - phones were tapped and anyway, he didn't want to answer a lot of where-have-you-been type questions right now. He would call her at the morgue tomorrow.

Chapter Ten

5:30 pm - Friday, September 12th
Hudson River - The World Yacht Cruise Line

Drew Sutton struggled to control his paranoia. It had been four days since his conversation with Mike Hagerty. He paced the parking lot of the World Yacht Cruise Line waiting for Ariella Serfis to arrive while his eyes swept the area; back and forth, constantly eyeing the arrival of each group, each couple, each person for any indication of a tail or surveillance. He had made the date with her by calling her at the morgue where the telephones were used by pathologists, deaners, secretaries, maintenance men alike -- a deterrence to any judge to issue an order for a wire tap lest an innocent person's right to privacy would be violated. A sit-down with Ari on a ship where hundreds of passengers would dampen any impulse to scream, cry, or become excitedly vocal would help, he thought.

The mid-September sun was setting on pier 81 at the foot of New York's West 41st Street and the cruise ship Inamorata tugged slightly at her mooring lines on the swell of a passing ferry. She waited patiently to load her cargo of romantics and sight seers for a dinner cruise around Manhattan. And Drew Sutton was a romantic. Plus he had a deep affection for Ari, one that developed over the weeks of steady dating and amore. He clutched his tickets and looked again at his watch. *This was going to be some evening.* One way or the other it would live brightly in the memory of them both. Drew's impatience grew in direct proportion to his paranoia. Boarding time was 6:00 PM and he had arrived early to detect any attempt at surveillance by the Feds. It was now 5:45.

Ari's entrance was as dramatic as any Act 1, Scene 1 appearance at the Shubert Theater. Her limo pulled within feet of Drew. She stepped slowly from the limo letting her leg slide out gracefully followed by her slender hips, shapely torso and a flip of the hand above her head. She was radiant, enjoying the occasion. Ari unfolded her 5' 7" slender frame, cocked her wrists, threw her hands in the air and twirled. The limo pulled away. Drew noted the license plate and driver's appearance and returned his attention to Ari. She was stunning: a black sheath dress, chiffon jacket, lightly shaded black hose and beautiful legs created the illusion. Drew was stunned.

"You like?" she teased.

"You know damned well I like," Drew grinned, "but I like it better without the trimmings."

"You'll have to wait, darling; be patient. You've done everything right," she beamed. "Let me take it all in. What a wonderful, romantic idea. A dinner cruise. In all the time I've lived in the city I've never been on one of these."

She was ecstatic and Drew tried to hide his discomfiture. He was running the risk of losing something precious and wished he could undo all this scheming -- play acting was not his best suit. He turned and took her by the hand. "Let's go, Ari or they'll leave without us," he fibbed.

"Wait," she tugged at his hand, spun him around and pressed her body against his, toe to lips. "A preview of coming attractions," she giggled and led him to the gangplank.

The orchestra's rendition of "New York, New York" guided the Inamorata from her berth at 7:00 and she sailed south on the Hudson to the end of Manhattan Island. Uniformed waiters served the happy throng. Drew and Ari were seated at a table for two on the starboard side. Drew ordered a bottle of Pinot Grigio and waived the usual ritual of taste and approval.

"When was the last time somebody refused a bottle of wine after tasting it?" he asked Ari.

"I don't know, really," she replied. "But let's just enjoy the cruise for now." She pointed across the dining room to the port side. "Look at the skyline. Doesn't it look just glittery and elegant in the sunset? The sun glints from the windows. Drew, I'm so glad we're doing this." There was adoration in her voice and face.

Drew melted. *I can't believe this is happening. I've built her up for what? Where are we going with this?*

The remnants of their appetizers of Chilled Gulf Shrimp had been removed and they waited for their entrée of Atlantic Salmon Fillet. The Statue of Liberty fell astern and the sight seers oohed and aahed at the sight of the lighted guardian of New York Harbor. A group of Japanese tourists stood erect in awe of the icon of liberty as the ship sailed around the tip of the island and up the East River.

Ari and Drew fell into a silence of wonderment at the sight of the underbelly of the Williamsburg Bridge. They finished the salmon and waited for their dessert of New York Cheesecake and a cup of Espresso. Turning under the Brooklyn Bridge, Ari reminisced.

"My Father used to say that Manhattan Island was anchored to the mainland by bridges."

She fell silent again. The table was cleared. Couples edged their way to the dance floor.

The ship was sailing a reverse course now and they had a better view of the city lights and buildings as they passed on the starboard. Ari and Drew now sat side by side. He had one arm across her shoulders and held her hand with his. She snuggled. They were spellbound as the ship sailed past the forest of concrete and steel - windows sparkling like shimmering silver leaves.

Drew broke the spell. "Ari, let's go up to the top deck. Let's feel the last of the summer breezes." He got up and held out his hand. The George Washington Bridge was the last sight on the trip and they would soon be turning underneath it. Drew had about a half an hour to talk seriously with her. Time was running out.

The breeze kept most passengers below but one couple lounged lovingly against the starboard railing. Drew eyed them. Big guy, 6'2", 250 pounds. Petite companion, 5'4", 119 pounds. They looked innocent enough. Drew tried to imagine them in bed. Ari stood at the prow, hair blowing in the wind, jacket flapping behind her -- a whaling ship's living figurehead.

Drew pulled over two deck chairs arranging them with one against the railing, the other facing it. "Sit down, Ari, I want to talk to you."

They sat facing each other. Their knees touched.

"You're not going to propose, are you, darling?"

It was a blow to the solar plexus of his conscience. They had sworn early on not to speak the three little words. *Now she speaks of proposing?*

"Don't tease. This is important." The gravity of his voice jolted Ari.

"Go on," she murmured.

The words poured out in a torrent. "You're being followed. Your phone is tapped. Your apartment is wired."

Ari paled. Her mouth hung open. "That's ridiculous. That's absurd. Why? You're can't be serious

"I am dead serious."

"By whom? What for? How do you know?" Ari was fast becoming agitated.

"The Feds -- DEA, FBI in conjunction with NYPD's narcotics squad."

"What on earth for?"

"They think your foundation is a money laundering scheme for the drug cartels."

"Who told you this?"

"A most reliable source."

Ari paused -- a wounded dove fluttering, plunging from her urban 21ˢᵗ floor aerie. "That's crazy, Drew. They must be stopped. They have no right. There's no truth to all this."

"Ari, they do this by court order. A judge signs such an order based on a police affidavit, which, by the way, lists evidence that convinces a judge for the need of such a surveillance. Good god, Ari, you've been around police long enough to know this. How many times has your autopsy protocol been used in an affidavit?"

Her defensiveness underscored her guilt; something Drew sensed immediately.

"What have I done; what is there about me to warrant such a search?" The injured dove was wheeling, turning, searching desperately for refuge.

"Well, I'm sure they're interested in your wealth. It doesn't fit a young pathologist's income."

"I told you, it's income from the foundation my Father set up for me. The apartment is part of a divorce settlement. Besides, how did they come to investigate me? I haven't done anything." She was on the edge, her speech shrill. Big Guy disengaged himself from Petite, turned and glared at Drew.

Drew turned up the heat. "Ari, listen. There was no divorce. There is no record of it or a marriage. And they probably started with Salinas and it led to you."

She seized the opportunity to take the offensive -- to turn the tide of the conversation. "So! You've been checking up on me. Is that it? Are you part of this?" Her rising voice pulled her from her chair. She flailed and threw her fist at him. Drew caught her by her forearms and levered her back into the chair. Big Guy started to cross the 25 feet between them. Drew held up his hand authoritatively, palm out -- stop. Big Guy hesitated, wheeled and grabbed Petite by one hand and pulled her down the stairs to the dance floor. *Many a tear starts to fall but it's all part of the game* drifted up through the stairwell.

"Goddam you, Drew. My one chance, my one attempt at real love -- yes, I said it -- love, and you screw it up. Couldn't you leave it alone? Couldn't you just love me as I love you?" The wounded bird fluttered once more and fell into an abyss of remorse and self-pity.

"Ari, listen to me -- I do love you but this isn't my fault. I didn't ask for this. I didn't plan this and I certainly didn't form this so-called foundation of yours. It is a drug operation, isn't it?" He fumbled for the right words. "But what I did do was violate my oath of office. I just tipped off a suspect in a crime. By law I'm obligated to report and act on any criminal information. I didn't -- I'm a cop non-grata. I could be arrested before you are!"

Ari swallowed the full import of his words, her eyes darting, searching for a retort, an escape. She found none. "Oh, god," she sobbed and dropped her face into her hands. "Drew, honey, I didn't start it. My Father left me this trust, this foundation, whatever the hell you want to call it. It was good for me. I was independent. It sent me to college to study what I always wanted to be -- a forensic pathologist. I loved it; I wallowed in it. I didn't need to marry anyone for money; only for love and you were the one. It was Andre Salinas, my Godfather, who turned it into a criminal venture. When I found out, I couldn't stop it; and I wouldn't if I could -- it was too good to me. I was wealthy; wealthier than my parents could ever have imagined."

"Was it Salinas who drove you here?"

"Yes. How did you guess?"

"Easy. That was no limo. No T&L tags. The driver didn't fit either."

"Drew what about us?"

The orchestra rendered *"Our love affair is a wondrous thing that we'll rejoice in remembering."*

"What about us, Ari?"

"You won't tell?"

"I can't do anything without implicating myself further. I've got to coop out somewhere until I figure this thing out. No, I won't tell. I won't have to, Ari; the Feds will move in before I take a second breath."

"Can you help me?" Her furrowed face begged.

"Ari, use that logic you learned at college," his voice quavered. "I would if I could. These past few weeks are not for nothing. But you don't need me. I would be an anchor around your neck. Co-defendants never wind up as friends.

The lawyers would play us against each other. Get a good attorney. That's what you need."

"Will I see you again?" Melancholy seeped from her welling eyes.

He looked away, down at the prow cutting the river. The once feeling of love and adoration, the warmth of her being, now turned to pity and regret - for her and himself.

They sat, silently, no words to express their anguish.

Ari rose and took him by the hand. "Dance with me once more."

Drew got up. "The ship is about to tie up. Just say goodbye."

"Once more; for old time's sake." She poured herself into his arms and clung to him.

The orchestra had put up their instruments. Sinatra's recorded voice prodded the lovers. *"There was a moon up in space but a cloud covered its face. I kissed you and went on my way. The night we called it a day."*

She turned to leave. "Ari, do me one last favor."

"Now you want a favor? After this you want a favor?"

He ignored the sarcasm but noted the tears running down her cheeks.

"Tell Salinas I have to see him. I want a contact. A big one. Not some street pusher. Someone who has some clout. Call him from the lab. Give him my personal cell phone number. I want this, Ari, please. Make him do it."

"I'll try. You could kiss me goodbye, you know."

It was not a lingering, sensuous kiss. It was firm, sweet, warm and meaningful. It told him she loved him and always would. She dabbed at her eyes, turned and headed down the stairwell.

Detective Sergeant Drew Sutton stood at the railing and stared at the black emptiness of the Hudson River.

Chapter Eleven

9:00 pm - Wednesday, September 17th
Staten Island Ferry Parking Lot

Det/Sgt Andrew Sutton was not a happy camper. The chill made the dark blacker. He was apprehensive – nervous. The humidity seeped through his blazer and his gray slacks clung to his legs. He ran his finger around his sweated neck and pressed the "light" button on his wrist watch. Five past nine.

An ugly voice had left acerbic instructions on Drew's voice mail; simple and to the point - "Bottom of the down ramp into the parking area under the Staten Island Ferry complex off South St., Staten Island. Nine sharp. Alone. No weapons. No company car."

He ran it over again in his mind. The tone was malevolent, sharp, and ominous. How much had Ari told Salinas? How did she convince him to show? Will he show? He pressed harder against the concrete retaining wall - trying to act nonchalant yet alert, casual yet vigilant - waiting for something to happen, surveying the area around him knowing he was being watched; unarmed and with no communication with anyone.

It happened quickly and quietly. The Lincoln Continental limo swung around the ramp curve and stopped almost at his feet. Before he could get a look, a powerful flashlight blinded and immobilized him.

"Don't move," the ugly voice again. *As if I have a choice!!* A pair of hands patted him, groped him from his shirt collar to his socks. *Hope you had a good feel, you bastard.*

The voice again, "Into the car." Sutton was firmly guided into the front seat. He was amazed at the expert and quick manner of his capture; obviously well practiced. They had done this before. With no dash lights, he was left with only a darkened profile of the driver. He dared not turn around. The car crept into the maintenance area of the lot and stopped almost as soon as it had started.

"Out," the voice growled once more.

Sutton stepped out of the car onto the service road running along New York Bay. He turned slowly and deliberately. No sudden movements his instincts told him. *Damn, what the hell am I doing here?* His role in the war against crime always had been well defined and simple enough. It's us against them - the good guys against the bad guys - we work for God; that kind of thing. No one ever challenged his authority. No one ever commanded him. He was the commander - he was the man in charge. But never any undercover crap, no sting operations. This was too much like Hollywood and he didn't like it.

Two figures oozed out of the back and bracketed him. "Okay, Mr. Salinas," the voice said.

A third man slowly and authoritatively emerged to confront him. The guy was big - in the shoulders - in the torso - in weight. He wore a heavy moustache; no other facial hairs. His silk suit shone, even in the dim light. Sutton braced himself. Somewhere, a boat horn bemoaned the night. Salinas looked him squarely in the face. "I'm told you want to see me." There was the hint of a snarl in his otherwise placid speech.

"Yes."

"Are you some kind of a nut? Who the hell do you think you are? Worse yet, who do you think I am?" His tone now dripped with an arrogant sarcasm that spelled serious trouble.

"You know who I think you are. You're Andre Salinas, Councilman from Brooklyn, and a Trustee of the Americans for Children Foundation."

Salinas' eyes bore into him. Sutton recognized power and ruthlessness when he saw it and what he saw now was the epitome of arrogant, ruthless, criminal despotism. He stared back.

"That's it?"

"That's it," repeated Sutton.

Salinas noted the omission of any criminal titles or activities. He paused, eyeing Sutton, mulling over his response.

"What can I do for you?" Salinas had made up his mind. "And hurry it up. We ain't staying here all night."

"I need somebody to set up an asshole."

"What am I supposed to do about that?"

"Point me in the right direction."

"Let's get to it, Sutton. These two friends of mine ain't had any exercise lately. You dick around with me and I'm going to get pissed. Comprende?"

Sutton noticed the mention of his name and had a good feeling about it. He grew bolder. "I thought you might know someone in the Florida area who could arrange it. I mean somebody; not some low life element." He was careful not to offer any criminal description.

"I mean some high level business man that can induce my target into a transaction where I can nail him."

Salinas took Sutton by the arm and led him away from the two gorillas. "Look, Sutton. You give me the impression of a smart guy. You treat me with respect and I appreciate that. You also are a good friend of a good friend of mine. Kabish?"

Sutton had no idea what was coming. He stood there nodding his head. *Had Ariella told him of the cruise? Probably. Then why wasn't he in the bay by now -- Salinas exudes the temperament of an alligator.* The landing lights of a descending plane briefly lighted the face of this powerful man. The warning horn of the last ferry from the South Street slips punctuated his last question.

"Under no circumstance," Salinas continued, "is our friend's name or mine to be mentioned. At no time is her name to be spoken - no matter what our future relations might be."

"Yes, sir." *Sir? What the hell am I saying?*

Salinas grinned. "You are smart. Even if you are a cop."

Sutton glared - jaw set; fists clenched.

"Easy does it," said Salinas. "Don't get your bowels in an uproar." He softened his tone. "Me and our friend's Father were pals, real close. Her Mother was Spanish, her Father Jewish. We became friends when he was a Provisioner. Know what that is?"

Sutton nodded with intense interest.

"He had twelve trucks supplying the butchers and restaurants in Brooklyn. You don't get that way without a little help. Know what I mean? I worked on the docks and unloaded the meat he cut up and processed for his customers. We were both pretty small time in our areas but became friends. He introduced me to some of his friends and soon I left the docks and ran for office. Made it with his help. I got him wired with some heavy hitting meat importers and things worked out. He married the sister of a Colombian friend of mine. Good marriage. They had a daughter, our friend." Salinas was deep into a narrative few had heard.

"I just about run the town and the docks. I made a lot of connections since her Father and me got hooked up. We made a lot of money. He died. So did his wife. They left a trust fund for our friend. Big bucks. He told me to take care of her; see she didn't piss it away. It throws off enough for her to live well and for us to have a foundation to help South American children."

Salinas paused to see Sutton's reaction. There was none. Salinas wasn't saying anything Sutton didn't know already.

"She is my God Daughter." Salinas spoke it with a reverent but ominous inflection. "We wouldn't want to see her hurt. Right?"

Sutton didn't blink. He said nothing. *Fate is a weird engraver on a tombstone.*

Salinas paused again to see if he made the proper impression. Sutton detected a hint of affection in his face at the mention of Serfis' safety.

"I'll never see you again," Salinas said. "I have your cell number. I'll see what I can do for you. Remember; our friend's name will never be spoken."

He grabbed Sutton by both arms and gently shook him with each syllable lending emphasis to his confession. His face clouded with misgiving. "She was a good girl. Smart. But I led her to the trough and she drank, just like I did. I just hope it ain't too late."

Salinas dropped his arms. He motioned to his two bodyguards and strode to the car. The car made off the way it came in. Silently.

Sutton never saw the brown paper-wrapped package being placed in trunk of his car.

Chapter Twelve

8:00 am – Saturday, September 20th
The King's Arms Motel

Drew Sutton snarked in the deep hole of a whiskey sleep when the incessant ring of the telephone fought to rouse him. His head throbbed and he groped for the phone, sliding it to his ear.

"Who is it?" he slurred.

"It's me, Eddy," his voice sighed in exasperation.

Drew sat up, head down, one hand to his forehead the other gripping the phone.

"Oh, no"

"Oh, no your ass. Come on, Drew snap out of it."

Drew's eyes were bleeding scotch and he tried to staunch the flow by keeping them at half mast.

"Where are you?"

"In the manager's office. I'm coming up."

Drew waited for Eddy on the edge of the bed trying to remember where he was and why. He eyed the half empty Dewars bottle on the stained night stand and groaned. Visions of some fleabag motel made their way through the murk. Aching eyes scanned the room - The King's Arms. Oh, shit. He raised his head and winced at the sun streaming through the slit in the dusty curtain.

Eddy threw open the door and Drew fell back on the bed. "Christ, Eddy close the door, the sun's killing me. How did you get in?"

"We raided this place three months ago, remember? In appreciation for the creative report about his lady guests, the manager just gave me a key. How did you get into this place?"

"Same way." The vortex in Drew's head was slowing down; he wasn't going down the drain after all.

Eddy brought out a thermos of coffee. "Trinken sie, mein Herr."

Drew shot him a look, sat up, sipped, sprawled out again. How did he get to this point in his life?

Eddy pulled up a fatherly chair and surveyed his partner. "Drew, how the hell did you get into this fucked up situation? The boss is looking for you; IA is looking for you, the Feds are looking for you. I've been looking for you. I figured you might coop out here. What the hell happened?"

"Don't know, exactly." The haze was lifting.

"Don't know, exactly? What the hell does that mean?"

"Where is Ari?" asked Drew.

"So that's it? This is about Ari, the forensic druggie? They scooped her up last night. She was laundering drug money. Did you know that? You were screwing a drug dealer," Eddy's voice rose. "They have a net out for anybody and everybody. They're turning the place upside down; inside out."

Drew moaned.

"You're into this up to your ass, aren't you? You knew about this, didn't you?" Eddy sat back sympathetically. "Drink your coffee, Drew. Give it up."

Drew cranked himself into a sitting position. He looked at Eddy – Eddy, his partner, the brother who was risking his freedom and career just by being here. He wiped his face on the bed sheet and grimaced.

"Last Wednesday night I met a guy; Salinas, one of the guys in Ari's trust fund for some phony-assed scheme to save the children in South America; only it was a conduit for drug money heading south. Anyway, I met him to see if he could hook me up with somebody to set up Dalton for a buy so we could grab him and squeeze him on the Chusinsky job. He had a couple of his goons with him and they tossed me and my car before they let me talk to him. We had our meeting but somebody must have been trying to set me up because when I got home I opened my trunk to get my running gear and I found a package on the floor. I took it in and opened it. It must have been a half a key of shit."

"How did you get a hold of Salinas?"

"Ari and I had it out. I found out through another source and confronted her. I asked her for the favor. A goodbye kiss, kind of." Sutton's brain was clearing. He took another sip and another. "Who made this bucket of horse piss?"

"It's working, ain't it? Keep talking," growled Eddy.

"Anyway, I figured I was being set up and flushed it – paper and all. Next morning I looked out and saw the trunk of my car had been broken into; it was popped open. They must have been using me to smurf the stuff out of the city for a pick up this morning. Then I noticed the surveillance cars. Three of them on the block. They must think I'm some kind of green horn. I know every car in the neighborhood. You couldn't miss them – they didn't belong."

"So who set you up; Salinas?"

"I don't think so. We were pretty straight with each other. Must have been one of his goons – or both of them – conducting a little business on the side figuring I'd never say anything or, not knowing, thinking somebody tried to steal my car."

"How did you get here?" asked Eddy.

"Went into the garage and got in the trunk of Aunt Katy's car. She drove me here. She won't say anything. How did you know about this?"

"I told you. Traxel's asking all over for you. Wouldn't say why but I saw him and the Chief in a huddle. It didn't look good," said Eddy. "You awake now? Know where you are?"

"Yeah, yeah, the King's Arms. Why? I'm not that hung over."

"The King's Arms? And where is the King's Arms?"

They both smiled at one of their old standards. "Around the Queen's ass" they chorused and snickered.

But it stopped as suddenly as it started. "Drew, you ought to see Traxel. Maybe there's something he can do to clear this up."

"You can't be as serious as you look, Eddy. They see me and they got me." Sutton thought back to Hagerty's warning. *They're going to rip you apart. You'll be pounding a beat or filing reports – if you have a job left.* "I've got to get out of here. I've got to see if I can get Dalton set up. I've got to do something to set things right or partly right before I walk in or they grab me. I'm still a detective and want to stay one; and I won't be if they grab me – even if they clear me."

"The longer you stay out, the worse it will be."

"I'll chance it." Sutton's voice was grim.

"Do me a favor, bro," There was compassion and commitment in Eddy's voice and a resolve. "Stay here until I call you. Here is a throw – away cell phone. It can't be traced. It's got ninety minutes on it. I'll call from a friend's house. I'll get Aunt Kathleen to pack you up a suit case and deliver it to our friend."

"Our friend?"

"Drew, shut up and do as you're told. You're not my Sergeant any more. It's like the old neighborhood, Bro. We're joined at the hip."

Drew dropped his head and yielded in silence.

"We may both be out of a job when this is done," Eddy said. " Can you support me and my family slinging hamburgers?" He opened the door, threw a wink at Drew.

"Now for chrissake, stay put," Eddy roared and left.

Chapter Thirteen

8:00 pm – Monday, September 27th
The Home of Professor Felix Calderon

Drew Sutton stared across the table at his opponent. Without looking at them, he picked up his cards and tapped them on the table into a neat pack, picked them up, and squeezed them into a small fan so that they peeked at him one from behind the other. He smiled. Four jacks, two nines and a deuce.

"I dealt; you go." He directed in a fake growl. "You, sir, are dead meat."

"Give me your twos."

Drew impolitely flipped his deuce to the grinning face.

"Lay down," the boy cried. "I win."

"How old are you, Jeff?" Drew asked.

"Eight."

"Well, if you want to see nine, stop cheating."

"I didn't cheat, Drew."

"Did so."

"Did not."

"Did so."

"Ma, Drew called me a cheat," the kid cried.

Penny Ancebia stuck her head in from the kitchen door. "Play nice, boys."

Drew smiled, reached across the table, grabbed Jeff behind the neck, pulled him close across the table and held him forehead to forehead. "I want to be your second at the next poker tournament," he grinned. "Besides, it's about your bedtime. Off you go and I'll see you tomorrow."

Jeff smiled and gave Drew a goodnight hug. "I didn't cheat," he whispered in Drew's ear.

"I know," Drew returned the whisper, "I was just rattling your cage."

Jeff trotted into the kitchen kissed Penny goodnight and ran upstairs.

Penny finished the dishes and brought in two ponies of Cointreau. "Thanks for being so good to Jeff," she said and handed a pony to Drew.

Drew waved off the compliment, "My pleasure. He's a good kid. You could do me a favor if you would."

"Shoot."

"Here is a written request for a 30 day sick leave. I spoke to Doctor Hipple on the phone. He said he would write me a note to cover the request. Give it to Eddy when you get back to town and have him pick up Hipple's note and submit both to Traxel."

"No problem"

"Thanks," said Drew looking around the library. "Who did you say owned this place?"

"My Uncle Felix Calderon. He is my mother's brother. We call him Uncle Cal. He's chairman of the Political Science Department here at Lehigh University. He's off on Sabbatical to London so I decided you could coop out here until things straighten out."

The words *I decided* did not escape him. "How long has he been in this country? I mean, I guess he's wasn't born here."

"No, he emigrated from Cuba early on and made a life for himself. Never married, just studied and worked his way through school. Loved it. Decided to stay in the education business. It was in his studies that he learned how the Castro regime was in trouble economically and sent word to my family to leave if possible. By that time I had been married and was about two months pregnant with Jeff. There were about 30 of us on the skiff. It swamped and 10 of us didn't make it. My husband, Roberto Sosa, was one of them. The Coast Guard picked up the rest. We came north to Elizabeth where my uncle took us in.

"But you go by Ancebia?"

"I kept my maiden name in the states. Don't know why; just thought it was the right thing to do."

Drew gazed in wonder at the revelation. What about Mom and Dad?"

"They moved to Miami. When Uncle Cal moved to Pennsylvania, they felt lonely and moved to more familiar environs."

"And you?"

"Jeff and I took our own apartment. But I can thank Uncle Cal for that. He had taken me under his wing. Helped with Jeff. Made me go to school and study, tutored me in everything. After high school, I took courses at Gibbs. I wanted desperately to get rid of my accent and fit in. Father Ignatius got me the job at the department."

"And here I thought of you as some fresh-assed babe off the block. Sorry for that. I'm deeply sorry."

"Don't. I deserve it sometimes. I got a big kick out of your remark one day about sex rearing its ugly head." Penny gave him a sidelong glance.

"Penny," Drew stammered. "I don't know what to say. You've been really good to me through all this. I certainly appreciate it but I don't understand it. You could get really jammed up over it."

"You're a detective and a sergeant and don't understand?" She rolled her eyes in mock wonderment and quickly changed the subject. "Look, Jeff and I are leaving tomorrow. It's an eighty mile drive and I want to get a good night's sleep. Let's just say goodnight and we'll see you again next weekend. The books are here in the library and the liquor is in the den."

She rose, took Drew's glass and went toward the kitchen. Turning she stared at him. "And besides, since when does sex have an ugly head?"

Penny turned, chuckled to herself and flipped a good night wave to a speechless Detective/Sergeant Andrew Sutton.

The Floater in the Kill

Part Two

Chapter Fourteen

7:00 pm – Monday, September 29th
The Offices of El Banco Norte Americano

Joachin Alvarez, his hands stuffed deep in his pockets, stared at the silhouetted Jersey City skyline, the receding western sun serving as an orange backlight. This was his place: the 51st floor conference room of the El Banco Norte Americano building overlooking the Hudson River from downtown New York City. It was a secure feeling reminiscent of the caves in the mountains of Cali where, as a boy, he sought solace, schemed, plotted, cursed his enemies and embraced his friends. Now he found himself at the pinnacle of success: Senior Vice President of the bank and also regional boss of the American arm of the cartel. No longer the cave man, no longer slouched in a jungle cave, but fifty one stories up watching the world move by train, by plane and ship, by car, truck and subway, and by electronic transfer of millions of dollars from his bank to the cartel. He slid his hand from his pocket to read the diamond studded $10,000 Rolex and turned on his heel waiting impatiently for his five *tenientes* to gather around the elliptical boardroom table. The cave man was plotting reward and punishment while he brooded over the sudden turn of events

Joachin turned back to the window and smiled to himself. This was his domain, his network. This is what he had worked for; what he had worked for from day one; what he had worked for from the day he arrived in New York as a sixteen year old sharp eyed, crafty kid working menial jobs, going to college and weaving himself into the fabric of big business in the big city. He had planned it early on and rewarded himself for the ten arduous years he had spent working at the bank. It was his to toy with - to tinker with until he perfected the network that sent the proceeds of the cocaine distribution ring to his *compadres* on the southern continent. He could set up financial accounts, send money in amounts unnoticeable to the Feds. It all started here and ended here; guarded by him and his cohorts. No one knew and no one cared. The $75 million a year, less his cut, passed smoothly and unnoticed through the electronic pipeline between New York and Cali.

A soft knock announced Jorge Martinez as he slipped through the heavy oak door into the room. Jorge Martinez, Vice President in charge of the seven New Jersey Branches of El Banco Norte. Quick witted and articulate in English, he anglicized his name and was better known as George Martin to the City and Council of Elizabeth, New Jersey. He had been elected easily as Councilman of the first ward by its Hispanic population and his council colleagues voted him Director of Public Safety. He oversaw the Police and Fire Departments and did a good job; did it efficiently and to the acclamation of his constituents. He was a clone of Alvarez, medium height, wiry with a quick smile and a firm handshake, he was astute and wily – another cave man.

Andre "Andy" Salinas followed him in.

"Hola," he grunted and gave an off-handed salute to the boss.

Salinas was the animal, the man quick to violence, shrewd and cagey - a danger to friend and foe alike. He was the shorter of the three and heavier. The enforcer, he had earned his calloused hands on the Brooklyn docks where his tough guy attitude and brutish ways earned him his place among the element. Now he sensed Alvarez's annoyance and displeasure. He waited and watched with darting, beady eyes. Yet he felt secure. After all, it was he who introduced Doctor Serfis and her father's "Foundation" to Alvarez and his crew making him eligible to join the El Banco hierarchy.

The three were joined by Ricardo "Ricky" Montano, boss of the Philadelphia area and Eduardo "Eddy" Comacho, in charge of the Camden, NJ distribution area. Both had been small time mid-level dealers and, with a little muscle got into the construction business and froze out other companies winning themselves contracts including those to build the local El Banco offices in their respective regions giving them the opportunity to meet Alvarez. They had gained their opening to the construction market by supplying the mob with cocaine in exchange for a small cut in their lucrative neighborhood businesses.

All five had established themselves and when he noticed some small money laundering transactions posted through El Banco, the crafty Alvarez put them all together in his larger, more profitable network.

George Martin, second in command, pointed to waiting chairs and sat down opposite Salinas. Alvarez turned from his window and with deliberate steps approached the group, sat at the head of the conference table, and motioned Martin to open the meeting.

Martin sat still. "Ari Serfis has been arrested," he said without expression.

Alvarez eyed the group looking for a hint of recognition. There was none.

"What happened."

A murmur buzzed around the table.

"All I heard from my source is that the Feds scooped her up last week. She is in the Manhattan Metropolitan Corrections Center."

Again Alvarez searched for a sign of knowledge. Some one must have known and he thought he knew who.

Salinas said nothing and scanned the table to mask any give-away facial expressions.

"Anything else?" Alvarez's tone drooled trouble.

"She tried to take her own life but failed. They found her with panty hose around her neck, cut her down and revived her."

Montano was incredulous. "How did she do that?"

Martin gave him a sidelong look. "Which word didn't you understand?" he spoke with agitation.

"I understand every word, wise guy. Why did she do it, how did she get the pantyhose? They take all that shit away from you in the lock-up."

"Somebody on the inside slipped them to her. She was upset, depressed. She lost everything: her cop boyfriend, she couldn't face us, she lost her job, lost her credentials – everything; a classic case of depression. She must have figured it was time to bow out."

Martin finished his report. "She is now under a suicide watch in isolation."

Alvarez got up and walked to his window. Flinging the words over his shoulder he rasped, "Salinas; she was your protégé. What do you know about this?"

"Not much, just what I heard now. I know she was seeing this detective from Elizabeth, but nothing ever came of it." Salinas responded. It was a cautious and elusive reply carefully avoiding the details of his contact with Sutton.

"That's it? That's all? Nothing more?" growled Alvarez spinning on his heels to face Salinas. Each word carried a threatening note. "What about this cop; what and how much does he know?" Alvarez was so enraged he reverted momentarily to his native language, "Ella le dijo algo a alquien?" *Did she say anything to anyone?*

All eyes now turned to Salinas who was sinking slowly into a quicksand of deception. The glare in their eyes joined Alvarez in his disdain for Salinas, the unthinking, lying muscle man.

"Can't be much. She wouldn't tell him anything." He said doubtfully. "All they were doing was playing house. She didn't know that much anyway."

His mind raced back to his conversation with Sutton. How much had he told Sutton anyway? Should have iced him right then and there, he thought.

Alvarez strode back to the head of the table.

"Georgie, what do you hear about this .. this .. this Sutton guy?"

"He's in the wind, boss," admitted Martin. "I overheard his Lieutenant and the Chief talking. I couldn't make it all out but it didn't sound good. I think they're looking for him quietly but can't find him. I heard Serfis' name dropped along with his. That's when I called you."

Salinas gulped. So that's how the boss found out. The quicksand was pulling harder now.

"Jesus Christ!" shouted Camacho pointing his finger at Salinas. "When Serfis goes to trial, they'll call Sutton. Maybe that's why they're looking for him; to prep him for trial. Then what? In my territory, we would have shot the son-of-a-bitch and tossed him into the Delaware, you asshole."

Camacho was screaming now to a chorus of the others.

Salinas rose to the challenge of his position.

Alvarez held up his hand. The room fell quiet to the sudden realization of what might be and to the command of the boss.

"There will be no trial." The words, like an arctic blanket, smothered all conversation.

"Salinas, see to it."

"But boss," Salinas pleaded. The implication was clear and fell heavily on the gathering. To Salinas it fell like an anvil. It wouldn't be the first time he had to silence a witness – but his own God-Daughter?"

Alvarez stared him down. "See to it. Comacho is right. Your stupidity brought us to this table. See to it. And Georgie, find that asshole of a detective."

No one paid attention to the trustee mopping the cells on the isolation floor of the Metropolitan Corrections Center. The time to clean the cells was during the ½ hour free time the inmates were allotted daily. No one saw him palm the little capsule to the depressed, morose, troubled Ari Serfis. She knew what it was and what she had to do – what she wanted to do. The trustee vanished as quickly as he had come.

The news item in the Daily News was brief.

"Authorities at the Manhattan Federal Correctional Center stated that a prisoner was found dead in her isolation cell Thursday at 7:00am. The cause of death is undetermined pending toxicology. A source close to the investigation who spoke on the condition of anonymity, noted that Ariella Serfis, a forensic pathologist employed by the New Jersey State Medical Examiner's Office, had been held on drug related charges. There were no signs of injury but, it was noted, her finger tips had turned blue. Dr. Serfis........."

Chapter Fifteen

2:30 pm – Thursday, October 2nd
Elizabeth, NJ, Police Headquarters

Lt. Traxel raised his eyes in time to see Jorge Martinez flit past his open door. *That's the second time today,* Traxel thought. *What is the Commissioner of Public Safety doing in my Detective Bureau?*

Traxel was innately suspicious, especially of political figures. He leaned back in his chair, chewed on the end of his pencil and picked up the phone. "Doris, come to my office, please," he said.

Doris McNamara, Chief Clerk of the bureau, stuck her head in the doorway.

"You called, Boss?"

"Yes, Doris, come in and sit down."

"What is it, Lieu? You sure look puzzled." Traxel had inherited his Chief Clerk when Lt. Quackenbush retired. She was loyal, meticulous, dedicated and focused on her work - things she got from her Father, a retired Deputy Chief long since deceased.

"Doris, how many times, that you know of, has the Commissioner of Public Safety visited the Bureau?"

"Gee, I don't know; I was here five years before you got your promotion – about 15 years, I guess. I've never seen him here. Why? Uh-oh. You just saw Martinez?"

"Yeah. What the hell does he want?"

"Beats me. I saw him talking to a couple of the guys. Couldn't hear much. He was talking to Eddy for a second. Asked him where Drew was; that's all I could hear. But I got this feeling he was snooping – you know how these guys operate; a little talk here and there, trying to pick up whatever news is available. A real snoop."

Traxel eyed her thoughtfully. "Do you know where Drew Sutton is?" His eyes were fixed on her face; scouring, searching for an unspoken reply..

Doris stared back; never blinked, looked up, down or away. "No, I don't; except he's on some sort of a sick leave."

"No kidding, Doris. I had to sign off on that, remember?" Traxel was irritated and frustrated.

"Geez, boss, don't take it out on me."

Traxel dropped his eyes. "Sorry about that."

"Is there a problem?" she replied. "I get the feeling Drew's in trouble here but no one seems to know or they're not talking."

Traxel paused, tilted his head back a moment then looked directly at her. He made his decision. "Close that door," he said.

Doris left the room and returned with a dictation pad and closed the door just hard enough to make the glass upper pane rattle. She returned to the side chair next to Traxel's desk.

"I thought this might be one of those off-the-record-don't-say-anything talks. This makes it look official to anyone passing," she said and crossed her knees, as if prepared to take notes.

Traxel smiled. "You're in the wrong end of this business. You should be working undercover in some bookie's office," he chuckled. "But let's get to it." He was about to breach the rules.

"I need to find Drew, Doris. His Ari, the M.E., was arrested and committed suicide in the Federal lock-up in the city. The Feds think Drew maybe was part of some laundering ring with her. They want to talk to him. I want to talk to him before they do. Can you keep a confidential ear out for me? It's important, really important."

"Gosh, Lieu, I don't think he's involved. It's not like him. A lot of us have heard about this thing but nobody's talking and I don't think anybody has any real read on this."

Again, Traxel looked directly at her. No sign or expression of duplicity. "Okay, but let me know if you hear anything. I don't mean to hurt Drew. I just want to know what he's up to. It'll be my ass along with his if he broke the rules – deliberately or otherwise."

He paused. "Tell Eddy I want to see him."

Eddy Nolan quietly closed the door and moved to the chair along the wall.

"Over here, Eddy, right next to me so we can talk." Traxel motioned to the chair Doris sat in moments earlier.

Eddy moved to the chair, sat and felt the warmth of the previous occupant. "What's up, Lieu?"

Traxel eyed him looking for nervousness or unease. He came straight to the point. "No bullshit, Eddy. Straight from the shoulder. What does Martinez want?"

"Beats the shit out of me. I haven't the faintest." Eddy was as calm as the outgoing six o'clock tide.

"Then let me put it another way. Where's Sutton?" Traxel gave him the glare that his Marine Sergeant used to give him.

Nolan got up and spoke as slowly and forcefully as he could under Traxel's glare and his own misgivings. "I honestly don't know and don't care. I know all about the M.E. and the mess she got into. I know all about Drew's bedroom gymnastics with her. I've heard it as well as you and I don't know anymore than that. Again, I don't know where Drew is and I don't want to get mixed up in this bucket of worms." He rose and went to the door.

"Hold up there, Detective." Traxel rose to his full height. "Let's you and me get this straight. I'm not out to hurt him. There are reasons — serious reasons - that make me ask. If you can help but don't want to, that's your decision but don't mouth off at me. Now, again, tell me what Martinez wanted. You owe me and the squad that much."

Eddy remained standing with his hand on the doorknob giving it an anxious twist. "Boss, Martinez wanted to know the same thing — 'How can I reach Sutton?' and I told him the same thing I told you. That's all that was said. I never spoke to him before and I expect not to in the future." He opened the door, left the room and quietly closed it behind him, thankful it had been closed during the conversation.

Traxel stared at the closed door and clamped the phone to his ear.

"Doris, get me everything you can on Martinez and that crazy — assed bank he runs. No Sam Spade stuff; just street talk. Don't talk to any of the boys about it. And when you do talk to someone, you just want to know because your uncle wants to park some dough. And Doris; ASAP, right?"

"You got it, Boss."

108

"By the way, you may want talk to Penny about this. She speaks their language and has contacts all over the street. But no one else! Tell her that, too."

Chapter Sixteen

8:00 am - Friday, October 11th
Lehigh, Pennsylvania

Drew Sutton maneuvered the aluminum lawn chair on Felix Calderon's back patio and adjusted the back rest to face the east. He lay in the chair absorbing the sun's warmth, inhaling the fresh air. He was in comfort's womb.

Half sitting, half laying, half dozing, half dreaming, he thought of the past three weeks and smiled in anticipation of Penny's next visit and grinned at the image of Jeff's playful yet serious nature – *a real nice kid and a really good mother,* he thought.

He could hardly wait. Especially today. The past few weeks were great and he waited in anticipation; a feeling of warmth rising in his being.

Drew got up and walked the campus he had come to admire; the library with the familiar textbooks with which he spent so many hours, the chapel where he found some relief from the nagging thoughts of his dilemma, the security office where he exchanged war stories with the campus Police Chief, a retired chief from a small town in middle Pennsylvania. He stopped at the student hall cafeteria for a bagel and coffee lunch and strolled in the warmth of the sun back to the oasis of his mind's desert.

He set the table for three and marveled at his domestic conditioning. Penny would be bringing something up for reheating for supper while he and Jeff played horseshoes in the back yard. He was accepted by all for what Calderon had explained him to be – a retired Naval Lieutenant which wasn't that far from the truth.

He was taking in the vista from the back picture window when the sound of tires on the driveway pebbles forced him to bound to the front windows and stand back to look out unobserved. What he saw made him spin to look at the mantle clock – 4:00PM. Penny was early and without Jeff.

Penny's smile and greeting could barely hide her consternation. And the pizza she carried in was not the usual dinner fare they had come to enjoy.

"Hi, Penny," he grinned. "Where's Jeff?"

"I left him with a friend - thought we might be alone this weekend," she replied.

Penny brushed by Drew quickly and headed for the kitchen where he caught up with her.

"Hey, hey," Penny, what's the rush?"

The words gushed from her trembling mouth. "Serfis was arrested."

"She what?"

"She was arrested." Penny blubbered. "She was in the Federal slam in the city and committed suicide."

Sutton was dumbstruck. "What else is there?"

"Traxel is looking for you. The Feds are looking for you; a guy – Martinez - is looking for you. The whole damn world is looking for you. Goddamit," she cried and flung herself at him and into his astonished arms.

"Hold up there, Penny," he said and untangled himself from her frantic clutch. He wrapped his arm around her shoulders and walked her to the living room. "Let's sit down and talk about whatever it is you're trying to tell me."

They sat down on the couch and Penny unfolded her story as neatly and quickly as she knew how – in typical police report fashion: no frills, no extraneous words, no embellishments. Drew managed a smile and joked. "Just the facts, Ma'am. Is that how it is?"

Penny slowly calmed down, took a deep breath and slouched against the back of the couch and exhaled, "Just the facts, boss."

He marveled at his sudden feeling for her; as if she were an essential part of his being. "Penny, I've never seen you so agitated," he whispered. "Relax, kiddo. The world isn't coming to an end. Let's reheat this pizza. Mushrooms and extra cheese; thin crust, I hope."

They sat opposite each other across the marble kitchen island.

"Do we have any beer?" Penny asked.

"No, but we have wine," Drew winked.

"How thoughtful," Penny smiled back, "What made you think of it?"

"Thank Uncle Cal," retorted Drew. "I found his wine cabinet."

"You sly devil, you," giggled Penny, her emotional trauma subsiding. "What kind?"

"Merlot."

"Ugh, makes me pucker."

They looked at each other at the implication and Drew quickly looked under the counter, unlocked the cabinet, pulled out a six year old Pinot Noir and uncorked it. "Not too dry, 'fruity aroma' as the experts say. Let it breath for a while," he said. "Stand by while I set up the microwave," Drew fussed with the appliance to give himself some time to think.

"There you go, it was still a little warm. I'll give it one minute. Let's talk. I have an idea who's looking for me, but who is this guy Martinez?"

"I don't know that much," Penny responded, "Traxel gave Doris the job of looking at him. He told her to bring me in on the detail and she filled me in; he said I speak his language. The guys in the DB have no idea of what's going on. Seems Martinez was asking Eddy about you and Traxel has got his nose really close to the ground on this one. We were told not to mention this to anyone."

Drew stared blankly at her as if peering into the depths of some mysterious black hole. "What does this Martinez do for a living, if anything?"

"He is the Vice President and Branch Manager of the Norte Americano bank on the Avenue. You may know him as George Martin, Councilman of the Second Ward and," she paused for emphasis, "he's also the Police Commissioner."

"Did you say bank? Norte Americano Bank?" Drew's eyes widened. The mention of a bank meant money; money meant legitimate money or laundered money. His mind raced. *Is he connected to the Foundation? Is that why he was asking for me? Did he know Ari? Does he think I have knowledge of Ari's so called Americans for Children Foundation?*

The buzzer sounded and Drew retrieved the pizza, deftly cutting it into eight slices. "It's a little soggy, but it'll do. Smells good anyway."

He looked across the counter at Penny. "That's it?" he queried.

"That's all I know. I got it from Doris. Haven't heard anything more in a couple of days. I really haven't had anything to do on the matter, anyway." She eyed him cautiously.

"Something's not right here," Drew said. "If he's legit, he wouldn't be pussy - footing around. He'd go straight to the Chief. I'd like to grab his ass and have a real good sit-down with him. What does Eddy think?'

"We worked it out so that he doesn't know where you are. What he doesn't know, he can't tell. We don't talk about you, and won't until it's right."

Drew thought it over. The silence was a long and welcome pause to Penny.

"I need to know something," her tone and expression told Drew it was serious.

"Go ahead."

"Is she gone; is it over between you two?"

"Who?'

"Who, who. What are you, an owl?"

"Lighten up, Penny. Who are you talking about."

"Doctor Serfis. She's dead; I know. But are you over it?"

Drew was astonished at her candor, her straightforwardness caused him to pause to make sure he was absolutely truthful in reply.

"Yes."

"It took you awhile to answer."

"Hadn't thought about it for some time. You made me think."

"And?"

"It's over. It's been over for some time, I guess."

'Good," she said matter-of-factly, got up, walked around the counter and kissed him on his upturned forehead.

The gas log burned and sputtered. The wine and warmth made them drowsy and they dozed on the couch in front of the fireplace. The wind freshened and the branches of an aspen brushed against the window. Penny awoke and slipped away from her euphoria. She eyed the mantle clock and gently shook Drew.

"Eleven o'clock, Drew; I'm going to bed."

He rubbed his sleep filled eyes and looked at her lithe form extricating herself from him.

"Alone?" It was a spontaneous question.

Penny held out her hand and raised Drew from the couch.

'God, Drew; I hope not."

%

Drew came down from the bedroom to the smell of bacon and eggs and home fries. It was seven o'clock and the sleepiness lingered. He saw Penny fussing at the grill and marveled at her form.

"You're up early," he muttered. "I'm ready for bed again."

Penny giggled, "Not today, sweetie; next time."

Drew smiled, walked over to Penny and hugged her. "Is it too soon to say I love you?"

"No, but only because I know you mean it." There was a note of finality in her tone.

Drew turned to hide his ecstasy and saw her packed bag at the door.

"Where are you going?" he cried.

"Sit down and let's eat," she said. "I'm going back home today because my friend can keep Jeff only one night."

"Sorry to hear that. Being alone with you and all that would have made for a glorious weekend. I was really looking forward to your coming up here. Tell Jeff I missed him."

"He'll be glad to hear that. He says to say Hello. And he'll be glad to hear about us. He wanted that as much as I did."

Drew's grin turned into a smile. "You two been plotting?"

"We'll never tell. By the way – and not to change the subject – Eddy gave me this note,"

Drew read Eddy's familiar scribble with consternation.

> *You remember Arthur Coulter? He was head of the Narcotics Unit and retired about 4 years ago. He says to have you visit him. He's Chief of Layton's Beach in FLA. Call him at 954-876-9292. It sounds important.*

"What the hell is all this about?" Drew asked.

"Beats me, dear. I didn't see the note and I didn't deliver it. Penny reached up and gave Drew a lingering, sweet kiss. "Goodbye, my darling, see you next week. Don't forget me." Penny got into her car and left, waving out of the window.

Don't forget me? She has got to be kidding.

Chapter Seventeen

7:00 am - Sunday, October 21st
Lehigh, Pennsylvania

A week passed. The cell phone rang 6 times before he could flip it open and press it to his ear and mutter an incomprehensible 'ullo.

"Wake up, Drew," the voice said. "Honey, it's me, Penny."

"Hi, what time is it. What day is it? Where are you?"

"Drew, I don't have much time. Listen to me"

"Wait a minute." He sat up on the edge of the bed and let his feet touch the scatter rug. He put the phone down trying to put things together and quickly put it to his ear. "Yeah, what's up?"

I'm in the laundromat. I can't talk long; there are too many people around."

"I'm okay. I'm listening."

"I spoke to Doris yesterday. She filled me in on what she had learned. Banco Norte Americano has its American office in New York City. The Senior Vice President and COO is a guy by the name of Joachin Alvarez. They have an affiliate office in Colombia; Cali, Colombia. It may even be the main office; but we don't know. The DEA has placed a bank guard on their payroll. About 2 or 3 weeks ago he took a list of names of evening visitors. Guess who was among them?"

Drew was now wide awake. "Tell me."

"Andre Salinas and Jorge Martinez."

"Is this the straight dope? Where did Doris get this from?"

"She had somebody in Trenton run the bank charter and she worked her way back from there to the Board members and executives. She gave the corporate stuff to Traxel and then he told her about what appeared to be a big meeting. We are now keeping an eye on Martinez locally. The Feds have the bank under electronic surveillance but the telephone lines are encrypted. They haven't been able to break it yet. Look, sweetie, I've got to go. There are just too many big ears here but it's the only place I felt safe to call you from. See you Friday night and I'm bringing Jeff."

Drew heard the click and the dial tone, gave the phone a quizzical look and flipped it closed.

He dressed absent-mindedly, had juice, toasted some frozen waffles, poured hot water over his instant coffee and mulled over the events while eating his breakfast; but he couldn't think logically – there was too much going on; too much to consider in order to reach a logical conclusion. Everywhere he looked his mind strayed - from bedroom to kitchen; from sun bathing to campus wandering. Too much relaxing; too much easy living; too much vacation. His mind had dulled like the edge of a rusting sword.

He grabbed a lined pad along with some number 2 pencils and headed for the campus library - his stride quicker and more determined than Friday's stroll. He crossed the campus green, past the admin building, past the bio lab, through the quadrangle. He took the library steps two at a time, pulled open the oak and glass doors and stopped at the librarian's counter. He asked her for permission to use one of the study group rooms, got a few pages of plain printer paper and headed for the rooms. On a Monday and at this hour of the morning, it was a safe bet study groups were still in bed recovering from the previous night's cramming. He selected a smaller room that had 3 tables – a large 6 seater with straight backed chairs; a round 4 seater with similar chairs and a group of cushiony lounge chairs around a coffee table. He avoided the urge to sit in one of the soft chairs – *for poets and philosophers*, he thought. What he had in mind was some serious thinking: back-straight--feet-to-the-floor type thinking.

He took the lined pad and listed those who were in some way part of his situation: Serfis, Martinez, Salinas, Alvarez, Coulter, El Banco Norte Americano, Hagerty and EPD. Next to each name he listed all he knew about them: occupation, address, age, nationality, location. Next, he laid out an association matrix on a piece of printer paper. In the middle of the paper he made a rectangular box and printed "bank" in the box. Directly underneath he placed a smaller box and wrote in Alvarez. He connected the boxes with a short, heavy line. Off to one side he placed a box marked Salinas; another box marked Martinez; another marked Serfis, another marked Coulter and another marked Sutton and another marked EPD.

Sutton drew a heavy line under the box marked EPD to Sutton and a heavy line from Martinez to EPD. Heavy lines were also drawn from Sutton to Serfis and another from Sutton to Salinas and another from Salinas to Serfis. From Serfis to the bank he drew a dashed line signifying an indirect association. He drew another dashed line from Martinez to Sutton. As an afterthought he drew a box for the DEA and connected the box to Hagerty and indirectly to Sutton and directly to the bank.

He studied the matrix. It was a simple thing but it allowed him to simultaneously reflect on who knew whom, under what circumstances, and the intensity of their association as compared to those of the others. And it became immediately clear: The DEA wanted to talk to him about what Serfis might have told him. Alvarez wanted to talk to him about what Serfis might have told him – but there's a good chance Salinas might have told him that already. And it looked as if Martinez wanted to finger him for Alvarez. This was the stuff movies were made of.

It also became clear he was the only person outside the money laundering ring that knew enough of their operation to become a problem to them, if not so already. That's why Traxel wanted him back and he couldn't go back because of his violation of judicial procedure on which his job now hung in the balance. And what of Coulter? Drew scanned and studied the matrix time and again and could find no connection with any of the listed entities to Coulter except the EPD. The note had come from Eddy; he knew that and thought of it again. *"You remember Arthur Coulter? He was head of the Narcotics Unit and retired about 4 years ago. He says to have you visit him. He's Chief of Layton's Beach in FLA. Call him at 954-876-9292. It sounds important."*

But something was missing. Why was Coulter hanging out there in the middle of the page with no connection to anyone except EPD? Sutton doodled. He drew a box, labeled it Florida and drew a heavy line to Coulter because he knew him to be in Florida. Next he drew a box and labeled it Dalton. Remembering Dalton's letter postmarked Florida, Sutton drew a line to Florida. *Of course! Chief Coulter probably knows about Dalton and knows where he is!* All thoughts of

Alvarez, Martinez, Salinas and company flew from his mind. He had Dalton in his sights!

Sutton picked up his things and went to the library pay phone to call Penny. He raised his hand to dial and hesitated; *was her phone tapped?* To avoid detection he called on his cell phone and left a cryptic message on her voice mail. "Pen; going to see the guy. Leaving ASAP. Will call on arrival. My best." He hoped her phone was not tapped.

Chapter Eighteen

11:00 am - Tuesday, October 15th
Layton's Beach, Florida

The Boeing 737 rode the glide path to Daytona Airport 2 miles south, its shadow on the ground slightly ahead; seemingly pulling it forward. Landing gear and flaps down, it dropped in its approach, skimmed the runway, eased gently to the asphalt, reversed engines and came to a roaring stop to the appreciative applause of the passengers.

The pilot wheeled the aircraft 80 degrees to the left and taxied to gate number 3 on the tarmac. Drew Sutton grabbed his carry-on bag off the overhead rack and joined the halting single file of anxious people up the aisle and into the terminal satellite. He scanned the bobbing, waiting faces behind the roped off visitors area until he spotted Arthur Coulter and headed in his direction.

Coulter wasn't hard to spot. A lanky six foot three, he had the sharp, leathery features of a West Texas sheriff with eyes brown enough to hide their pupils. His grin seemed menacing and artificial but when he smiled broadly, he appeared genuinely bright, happy and humorous. Drew reached him and shook hands with the former Elizabeth Police Captain.

"Hi, Cap, long time no see."

"Chief, to you, my man; and don't you forget it," quipped Coulter. He took Drew's hand and gave him a playful left hook to the chin. "Give me that bag."

Coulter snatched Drew's bag and guided him to the powder blue and white Ford Crown Victoria prominently marked "Layton's Beach Police."

"Jesus," Drew remarked, "Who picked out the colors, the Ladies Garden Club?"

"Get used to the colors down here, smart ass; it's what's inside that counts," Coulter smiled.

Chief Coulter was right. It's what's inside that counts and the ride to Layton's Beach proved it. Drew was awed that these small departments had the equipment they did: up-to-date in almost every aspect and he told him so.

"We have a department of about 7 men including myself, but we handle it well enough. Our biggest problem is drugs, of course. We're in that area where they love to drop their bundles and beat it. Comes in by boat in the ocean and dropped overboard in waterproof bundles that float in or are picked up by smaller craft and distributed," Coulter explained.

"And how do you know when these shipments are to arrive?"

"Well, I've been lucky and cultivated two good snitches."

"Just like old times?"

"I guess," shrugged Coulter.

They pulled into a heavily shaded street and then swung into a cobbled drive for about 500 feet that led to a low ranch with large overhanging eaves. A heavy smell of salt water told Drew the Atlantic couldn't be that far away.

"Here 'tis," grunted Arthur, swinging his long legs out of the car. "The old homestead. Go ahead, I'll get your bag."

Drew paused at the sign hanging from a cedar post at the head of the walk. "Tiki" it said and he headed for the screened patio where a striking woman appeared in the door frame. "Hi, you must be Drew Sutton," she said and shook hands firmly. I'm Mary Simpson, Art's wife. In case you're wondering, we call this place "Tiki."

Drew smiled, "I noticed."

"Look out for her, Drew, don't let that beauty mesmerize you." Art had come up behind him. "She's a former DEA Special Agent and can handle herself. She's handled me for twenty years." He leaned over and gave her an affectionate kiss. "In case you're wondering, she kept her maiden name for security reasons."

Drew felt a sudden unease. A former narcotic strike force Captain and now a former DEA agent. *Is this someplace I want to be?*

"Lunch is ready, boys. What can I get you to drink?"

Drew smelled fried fish and French fried potato slices and quickly said, "Beer."

Lunch was quiet and leisurely yet somewhat quick. Drew didn't speak until spoken to and waited for the subject of Serfis, Dalton and such to arise.

"Let's you and I take a stroll through the house and grounds," said Art. The offer was more a command than a suggestion.

Drew was impressed by the simple elegance of the place. It was built in a broad "U" shape with one leg containing the bedroom and retiring area for the Coulters and the other for guests. In the cup of the "U" was a canopied in-ground swimming pool in the middle of a Polynesian type garden. Doors from each leg gave access to the pool area. Art flicked a couple of switches to show off the lighting scheme.

"In case you're thinking about how a retired police captain can afford something like this, Drew," Art volunteered, "Mary and I are both retired with no children. We both have good pensions and have been saving for this for years. My job as Chief keeps me out of her kitchen and is nothing more than beer money. But it's in my blood." He grabbed Drew's arm, pointed out his room, and led him to the back yard.

It was about one hundred fifty feet from the house to a portion of the inland waterway canal. "We can sit here and wave to folks on board watercraft that go by – sails, motors; all types. Here, pull up a chair," Art said.

They sat side by side and took in nature's allure. Drew took it all in, the lushness, the calm, the serenity and found himself fantasizing about Penny and Jeff.

They heard the squawk of a group of sea-gulls. "They follow the fishing boats in," said Art. "Just don't look up," he grinned.

"Don't have to," said Drew and pointed to a black and white gull hopping about the grass, eyeing them.

"Looks like the damn fool is wearing a Tuxedo," laughed Art.

Drew sat up, wide eyed. "Well I'll be dipped in shit and called a turd," he exclaimed. "Tux."

Coulter gave Drew a sidelong glance, raised his eyebrows and stared at another fishing boat making way through the canal. They sat in silence for a moment one waiting for the other to broach the subject.

"Art," said Drew without looking, "I'm here at your suggestion. What do we talk about?"

"I hear you are looking for a guy that killed someone in a bar in Linden."

"Not recently," Drew responded. "Who told you?"

"Bernie."

"Bernie?"

"Bernie Traxel. We talk every now and then. You know, just to keep current."

"How much has he told you?"

"Just about everything. Serfis, Martinez, Dalton, El Banco."

"Does Traxel know I'm here?" Drew was getting anxious.

"I never told him. I invited you. Look," continued Coulter, "I called him with what I thought was information he could use. "Your personal problems are of no concern to me. As a matter of fact, I find them rather intriguing but still none of my business."

"How did you find me?"

"Traxel told your partner about my information, said you were on sick leave. Nolan called me. The next thing I know, you call me. Now let's have it. All of it."

Drew took a deep breath and told Coulter the long sordid tale – Serfis, Chusinsky, Dalton, Salinas, all of it. "That's it," he said finally.

Coulter turned in his chair and looked Drew in the eye. "Dalton is here." Drew was dumbstruck. "How the hell did you find out?"

"That walking piece of shit is going around talking to my snitches about how he got away with icing somebody up in the Elizabeth area. He's trying to impress everybody and trying to muscle in on the local trade. I spotted him the minute he landed here - remembered him from up north. He's been under surveillance ever since. That's why I called Traxel; asked him if he knew anything about it."

The dinner bell rang from the house. "Look, let's let this rest for tonight. Have a good dinner. Mary and I have an engagement tonight. The place is yours. The liquor cabinet is in the den and the phone works. TV works, too and the VCR. The pool is open. If you're going to skinny dip, do so before ten; that's when we get back.

The bell rang again. "Let's go fellows, dinner." Mary shouted.

Chapter Nineteen

8:30 am - Wednesday, October 16th
Layton's Beach, Florida

Drew woke to the aroma of coffee and lightly toasted Belgian blueberry waffles. He yanked his arm from under the covers, peered at his wristwatch and crept to the open hallway door peering into the garden. Mary and Art were lazing over their cups and toying with their waffles, speaking in low, serious, intimate tones. Drew retreated, yanked on his pants and shirt, shaved, brushed his teeth and strolled into the pool area.

"Morning," he said, "How was the evening?"

Art leaned back and threw a good morning back at him over his shoulder, "Not bad. How about yourself?"

"We have a bathing suit in the guest closet if you want to take a dip before breakfast." Mary said.

"Thanks. Can I trade it in for a good cup of coffee?"

"There's a rule in this house: if you're here for more than 10 minutes, you're no longer a guest," said Art. "Help yourself – coffee, waffles, juice. Make yourself at home."

Drew sipped his orange juice and looked over the rim of his glass at them. Mary seemed preoccupied; Art thoughtful. Something was up. He had his breakfast, leaned back and looked from one to the other expectantly.

"Drew," said Art deliberately, "we spoke to some people last night about your situation…."

Drew rose from his chair as if he were about to leave.

"Sit down," scolded Art, "this should be of benefit to you. The people we spoke to have no interest in you and you may never see them. So relax."

Art sat up in his chair. He looked tall even sitting down. "Last night you spoke of setting up Dalton. Well, he's starting to become a pain in the ass to me, too. I'd like to get rid of him before he creates a real problem for me; right now I'm just keeping an eye on him to see where he might take me. He hasn't done anything that would lead to a big bust but I don't want anyone getting hurt because I didn't act in a timely way. Understand?"

Drew nodded uneasily. He spotted Mary in the kitchen on the phone.

"Have something in mind," he asked.

Coulter noticed his apprehension. "Look, Drew; I was led to believe this has become some sort of a quest for you. If this is nothing more than revenge, forget it; it rarely works in your favor; revenge often obscures reason. On the other hand if this is some kind of maneuver to nail a scumbag and throw his ass in the slam, that's another matter. Some would say it might even be good police work."

Mary appeared in the doorway and nodded to Art. He nodded back.

"Now, as to your internal problems with Bernie and company. Forget it. You're off the hook. I have it from a very reliable source you probably did little more than to get him pissed off – which is bad enough. It may not be evident to you, but he thinks you're okay – just need a little dusting off as they say.

Drew eased his grip on the chair.

"If the Feds bust Alvarez and his crew, you'll probably be called at which time you'll have to work your way out of that situation yourself seeing as how you didn't go to Bernie and them right away. You're supposed to act quickly on any knowledge of a criminal act; right?"

"You're not telling me anything new." Drew glared at Coulter. He couldn't wait for the end to the lecture.

"Don't get testy. Are we working for the same thing here?"

Drew softened. "What do you have in mind?"

"You said that before." Coulter grinned broadly and they both pulled closer to the table.

Coulter's plan was simple: His informant would suggest to Dalton where he could get a big supply of coke to further Dalton's enterprise. It was simple enough; the informant would direct Dalton to the big guy and would tell Coulter when and where the meet would take place. When Dalton came back with the dope, they would nail him.

"Who is they?" asked Sutton.

Coulter leaned back and pushed his chair away from the table. *Uh-oh* thought Sutton who read the body language to mean there was a surprise, a hitch coming.

"Look," Coulter replied, "We can't pull this off by ourselves. We need some manpower and some jurisdictional authority. You can't make an arrest down here, can't even pull your weapon under most circumstances.."

"Are you taking this away from me?" demanded Sutton. "Are you telling me that I'm out of the picture? Is that what Mary has been doing all morning?"

"Don't get your bowels in an uproar. The short answer is no. You'll get credit for the grab. The other part is Mary has been getting her old boss and the Coast Guard lined up in the event this thing comes down."

"And the Coast Guard how would they fit in?"

"Listen, Drew; you're a homicide guy. I've spent years on this narco shit. What's more, I'm Chief of this burg. I want this switch to take place on the water. Nobody gets hurt and Dalton won't have any place to go but ashore where the gendarmes will be waiting. And you'll be with me all the way. You dig?" Coulter was getting steamed.

Sutton looked glumly from Art to Mary and back. "Sorry. But I've been hoping and looking forward to the day I nail this creep. Never had the chance to think it through."

"Good," shouted Coulter, "We're agreed."

"Hold it. Not so fast. That takes care of your end; but what about the homicide? What the hell would we extradite him for? What do we charge him with?" moaned Drew. "We have no case against him."

"My snitch will testify Dalton bragged to him about the murder."

"That's it? One snitch with probably a sheet as long as your arm is the only witness? We have to do better than that."

"Don't sweat it. Once the witness testifies to the Grand Jury you can hold him while you put the rest of the case together," explained Coulter, "And if that doesn't work, the DEA will charge him. Either way it's a slam dunk."

"What makes you think Dalton will go for it?"

"Greed, my man, greed. I know his type. He's a sleazy – assed junkie. A street dealer who thinks he's ready for the big time."

"And what about the supplier?"

"The Coast Guard will grab him when he leaves the area. We have set that up, too."

"You're the boss."

Coulter and Sutton stood up and shook hands. "Look. Drew, there's fishing gear in the garage. Here are the keys to the beach buggy. Why don't you go down to the beach and try your luck. It'll be some time before this thing starts rolling. Enjoy the time while you can. Things will happen soon enough and when they do – be ready."

Chapter Twenty

10:30 am - Wednesday, October 27th
Daytona Airport, Florida

Al Dalton never expected to see the Learjet parked in hangar #3. In fact, he had never thought what to expect. Just meet this guy in the gray, short Caddy limo at the foot of the fishing dock in Layton's Beach the voice had said and he would be driven to Daytona to meet the Boss, the Jefe, El Grande, and a deal can be made.

Now he stood at the open doors to the hangar where he had been let off only to look at the slender nose of a magnificent aircraft. It represented more than aerodynamic beauty. To Dalton it drooled money, all forty three feet of it; the GE CJ610 jet engines tacked onto the fuselage, the thirty five foot wingspan all smacked of twenty dollar bills. He could taste the green and he gloried in the image of the pool of money in which he would soon be swimming.

He gathered up the full length of his six feet two inches and strode toward the man walking under the fuselage.

"Nice plane," said Dalton acting nonchalantly and not knowing what else to say.

The man turned and measured Dalton from head to toe. "What can I do for you?"

"This is hangar 3, right?"

An imperceptible nod.

"Supposed to meet a business associate," Dalton crowed, "name's Al Dalton."

"This way," and the man led Dalton to the stairs to the plane's passenger cabin. Dalton started to climb them eagerly when he noticed two thuggish bodyguards at the plane's hatch watching his every move. He halted, started slowly and, reaching the top, began to brush by them. Arms sprang up and blocked his path. When the arms lifted, the loose jackets revealed 9mm Berettas in hanging shoulder holsters.

"Halto," one said. They other ran hands and fingers over Dalton's frame.

"Follow me," the other said and led Dalton into the passenger cabin.

Humberto Rios sat on the gray leather divan across the rear of the cabin. Slight, mustachioed, middling tall, his piercing eyes took in Dalton's bravado and he smirked inwardly. "Please be seated," he said and made a sweeping motion toward the four single seats facing him.

Dalton felt uneasy. This man was not what he anticipated and Dalton was losing his high handed attitude. He sat down without a word, the two henchmen on either side.

"So, you are Big Al," Rios smiled, "What can you do for me?"

Dalton was taken aback. "Well, wait a minute. I came to see what you can do for me."

Looking straight at Dalton, Rios said to his bodyguards, "Tengan cuidado con este hombre. El as un peligro. El cree que el es Dios." *Look out for this man, he is a danger. He thinks he is God.*"

"Senor Dalton, I am a busy man. I don't do things for people - they do things for me and sometimes I help them. Let's not waste time. You are a two bit street pusher with a bar from which you deal. There are many like you and I sell to them. In case it has escaped you, this is a business, a cash business."

Dalton shrank from this stinging rebuke. "I have the money," he said.

"I'm not so sure," responded Rios, "I know you had a bar called 'The Haunt.' I also know you had another 'The River of Gold'. Both sleazy topless gin mills. I have looked at your bank accounts; not so good, yes? You have business accounts at El Banco Norte Americano, Si? And the local police departments aren't too happy with you either."

Dalton's jaw dropped. *That was a while ago*, he mused. *How does he know these things? How did he get those figures?*

"Now, Mr. Big Al, what can you do for me and maybe I for you?"

"I have a market and need a better supply.

"And what is better?"

"I need 5 keys."

"Impossible. You don't have $250,000. I know you, Mr. Dalton, don't take me for a fool. You don't own a suitcase big enough to carry a thousand in 100 dollar bills."

"How about 4 keys."

"You want to buy 4 keys; is that what you are saying?"

"Yes."

"That's $180,000. How soon?"

"Two weeks. I can put the money together in two weeks."

"It's a deal. Mr. Chavez here will make the arrangements."

Chavez lifted Dalton from his chair and guided him from the Learjet. Inside the limo Chavez gave him his instructions: In two weeks, on November 10th, Rios will have his boat idling off shore of Layton's Beach about a half mile out. Dalton is to take a dory with an outboard to meet him there and make the exchange. No one, but no one, is to accompany Dalton. He is to come unarmed with no running lights and the cash; all of it. If he is not there at 9 pm, Rios will leave the area and Dalton will be a marked man.

"Comprende?"

Dalton was beside himself. He had dealt drugs for years; he was a user – could snort a couple of lines with the best or worst of them – but he never had he the prospects of having so much merchandise at his disposal before. The gods were good to him. He was rich.

"I'll be there – bank on it."

Chapter Twenty One

8:45 pm – Monday, November 10th
The Atlantic Ocean

It was a Hollywood night – a cloudless sky, the moon in its first quarter and the tide slowly starting to run to shore on a quiet sea. At 8:45 pm Humberto Rios and his sidekicks, Alva Chavez and Sergio Castro, waited in the cockpit of the Midnight Express for Al Dalton and his money. They sat quietly listening for any sound that would signal his approach. The boat rocked on the gentle swells of the incoming tide and dipped into their shallow troughs. The exhausts of three 225 HP Mercury outboards gurgled, mindless of the 30 gallons per hour it would take to escape the area at 70 miles per hour.

On shore Coulter and Sutton were stationed with night vision binoculars and walkie talkies in a tower atop an abandoned Coast Guard Station waiting for Dalton to make his move. Four DEA agents were spread out along a half mile portion of the beach.

Dalton was spotted simultaneously by Coulter and Chavez. He was driving an old Chris Craft and was half way out to the Midnight Express.

"There he goes," whispered Coulter into his radio. He was answered by four "10-4"s.

Dalton pulled alongside the Midnight Express, dropped his bumpers between them and clambered into the cockpit with an attaché case of neatly wrapped one hundred dollar bills. Rios smiled. "Sit down," he told Dalton and nodded to Chavez. "Count it."

Chavez snatched the case and opened it in one easy, practiced movement. He stopped counting and looked up at his boss.

"How much?" muttered Rios.

"One hundred thousand."

Rios turned his head to Dalton. "Where's the rest?" his voice dark and ominous.

Dalton was cool and arrogant. "I couldn't raise it all in two weeks. You can trust me, I'll have the rest in a week. Ask anybody; I have a good reputation."

"I'm not asking anybody. I'm asking you. Where's the rest of the money? Do you take me for a fool?"

Dalton could feel the breath of the dragon. "Look, Rios, I told you I would have it in a week. I'm not some jerk-off street pusher. This is Al Dalton you're talking to." Dalton started to rise from his chair. The years of cocaine, marijuana and booze rose in a bombastic tirade of hot air.

Castro grabbed Dalton by the shoulder and pulled him back into his seat.

"You are a dead man," growled Rios.

Enraged, Dalton slipped from Castro's grasp and lunged at Rios, punching him in nose and driving his nose bone into his brain. Rios died instantly.

Chavez and Castro instinctively pulled their Berettas and fired a fusillade into Dalton that dropped him in a bloody pile on the floor, picked up his limp body and threw it over the side.

The sound of the helicopter jarred them from their shock and they picked up Rios, dumped him overboard and roared off to escape the Coast Guard searchlight.

Sutton saw the muzzle flashes before he heard the volley of shots. "What the hell was that?" he cried.

"Beats the shit out of me," Coulter said, "Dalton's boat is out there bobbing on the swells and Rios' boat took off like a shark going for his supper."

They looked at each other, the questions hanging in the air.

"I don't think we're going to see Dalton for a long, long time," said Coulter.

Sutton kicked the wall of the derelict look - out tower.

"Shit."

Chapter Twenty Two

7: 00 am – Thursday, November 13th
Layton's Beach, Florida

Squatted on the beach, Drew Sutton poured sand from hand to hand and watched it trickle through his fingers unaware of the old man standing slightly apart from him. Squinting against the reflected sun, he searched the sea mulling over the events and wondering where he made the mistake fatal to his case. He was trained in the law and the search for truth. He practiced his training and was good at it. He mostly enjoyed his work – the highs and the lows; frustrations and successes - and knew well the pitfalls of allowing personal emotions to enter an investigation.

"What's up?" asked the man.

Drew turned his head and looked at a pair of gnarled knees attached to worn legs sticking out from under a pair of tattered khaki Bermudas. He also spotted a black Lab whose beady eyes laughed at him. Instinctively he held out his hand, palm up. The Lab took the invitation and pounced on him, knocking him flat on his back.

"Hey, you big galoot," shouted Drew, but the dog straddled him, licking his face and hands.

"Jake, sit!" commanded the grinning man while extending his hand to help Drew up. "Sorry 'bout that," chortled the man. He's really a big kid, playful and all that. "Name's

Holman Dance; call me Holmy," and he yanked Drew to his feet.

Drew grunted. "Andrew Sutton; call me Drew."

They shook hands and Drew found himself peering into the face of a 75 year old salt; furrows of character lining a face that held a simple, friendly smile and a pair of gray eyes; wise behind their twinkle. They walked slowly up the beach to the high water mark and sat on a large creosoted log of driftwood.

"Been watching you for near onto thirty minutes, Drew. Got a problem?" queried Holmy.

"Nothing you want to hear; nothing I want to talk about."

"Now that's what I mean. A man's troubled when he answers like that."

"It's a police matter," said Drew with a note of finality.

Holmy looked out to the sea. The breeze felt good; the salt air refreshing.

"So you're either a cop or on the lam."

"All of the above. What about you?" Drew wanted desperately to change the direction of the conversation.

Holmy leaned back against an abandoned piling. "Retired. Was a merchant seaman during the war. Retired to Lighthouse Keeper at the Cape and retired again to beachcombing now-a-days. Love the sea; sailed all over. Been there, done that."

"What war?"

"The big war. The righteous war. WWII."

Drew rose and arched his tired back. He thought of his mother and her journey after that war. Yet his thoughts wandered elsewhere. *If only he hadn't taken up with Ari. If only Chusinsky hadn't been in the Kill for a week; if only the body would have been found at the scene; if only some trace of evidence had been found – fingerprints, a weapon, witnesses, anything. Yes, and if the dog hadn't stopped to take a shit, he'd have caught the rabbit.* He kicked the sand, spraying his frustration into the onshore breeze.

"Let's take a stroll," suggested Holmy. If we don't get down to the shoreline soon, ole Jake will come up and drag us down there." *This kid needs his head cleared,* he thought. He also wanted to be alee of any more wind blown sand.

It was too early for most beachgoers and Holmy and Drew walked slowly in silence. Some sea-gulls dropped to the ocean's surface fishing for food; some dropped to the sand to pick at whatever old man sea washed up: sea crabs, mussels, dead horseshoe crabs, conches. Ahead, a flock swirled, swooped, dipped, rose on the wind.

"Watch Jake," Holmy said. "He loves to chase those birds."

"He sure does," replied Drew. "What's he jumping at?"

"Beats me. He's always playing with something – a real big kid."

Jake was barking and stalking something at the waters edge. It rolled in the gentle surf – moving up the beach with each nudge of the incoming tide. Jake leaped forward and backward with each advancing and receding wave. Holmy quickened his step. War had shown him something like this several times before.

They arrived to find what appeared to be a large pile of soggy clothing. Jake looked at Holmy pleadingly – *Help me with this thing.* A sea-gull was perched on the pile of rags teasing Jake, keeping him from jumping on it.

Both men recognized the shape of a dead body and ran to pull it ashore. Jake backed off looking from one to the other in puzzlement. The gull refused to leave its perch, its white chest, white head, black wings defying the onlookers until Holmy rolled it over to see its face. Al Dalton!

"Al Dalton, you magnificent piece of flotsam," shouted Drew.

The gull screamed, circled Drew's head, and rose skyward.

"You know this guy?" asked Holmy.

"Yes," said Drew. He watched the bird and murmured, and I know that gull, too. It's Tux."

"Tux? What the hell is tux?"

Drew didn't answer. He stared, dumbstruck, at the pile of soggy flesh and clothing.

"Son," said Holmy patting Drew on the shoulder, "you have more troubles than I imagined. You guard the treasure. I'll get the gendarmes. Tux? Well, I'll be a son-of-a-bitch."

He shook his head, gave a farewell nod and ambled up the beach.

///

Drew twirled his Bloody Mary in the circles of water on the bar and stared blankly from the veranda of Art Coulter's home. The mid-day sun pierced the canopy of transplanted Hawaiian palms that gave the place with its Tiki bar a Polynesian illusion. He was contemplating his navel.

He was jarred from his muddled thoughts when Art let the door slam. "Afternoon Drew," he said, "deep in thought?"

Drew offered a muffled "uh huh. "

"Well, it's done with. He took at least 10 shots; all in the body. A quick check shows two weapons: both 9mm. Have you heard from Rios?"

"You don't really think I will, do you?" Drew asked incredulously in a retort tinged with sarcasm.

"Hey, just asking. Loosen up, kid."

"Sorry, Chief. But this didn't go as planned. I wanted Dalton but not like this; not like a sieve. I wanted him in jail. I wanted to squeeze him. With him in the slam I wanted anyone who knew about Chusinsky to roll over. Know what I mean? I wanted him in jail while we built our homicide against him."

Art Coulter sat back and stared at Drew. "It won't matter now. And besides, the incentive may be greater with him dead but it doesn't matter; the case is closed. Who knows; maybe nobody would have come forth with him alive – in or out of jail."

"The case may be closed and justice may have been served but Mrs. Chusinsky is cheated. This thing will be lost in the obits up north. No trial; she won't gain any satisfaction from the press – no headlines about her son's killer being caught. No ......," Drew trailed off staring at a group waving from a passing 30 foot Wellcraft. "And what about me? Nobody's going to give me a shred of credit in this thing – nada – bupkus. I'll still be the guy who screwed the pathologist smurf and got bounced for it. And she's with the fishes just like Dalton and Chusinsky, not doing me a damn bit of good."

"What did you come down here for anyway, Detective? Social justice? Closure for a woman who raised a junkie low life? Maybe personal revenge because of a tarnished reputation or because you were cheated out of a bunch of high fives and 'good jobs'? And, oh, excuse me, maybe devotion to duty – one less open case for the department?"

Drew thought and looked up at Coulter. "All of the above."

"Man, I know what you need and it's none of the above." Coulter headed for the garage. "And I can't help you with that," he shouted. "Sit there and mope, if you want. I'm going fishing."

"Hold up, there, Art. Don't get carried away," shouted Sutton. "I know what I need. I need a favor."

The thought of the last few days' activities had built up in him; built up to a point where he needed to talk to someone, confide his feelings to someone; someone a little more sensitive to his feelings - he needed Penny.

"What is it," grumbled Coulter.

"Would you mind if I had company down here for a couple of days?"

Coulter eyed him warily, then smiled. "I thought so." He hesitated, "Do you want us to take a short trip? Do you want the place for your own for a time?"

"No, Art. I'd like some one to talk to; I need that someone. And besides, I want you all to meet her. It's time I brought her out of the closet."

Coulter thought for a moment. "Is it for real?"

"I think so."

"Then go for it." And Coulter clapped him on the back.

Chapter Twenty Three

11:30 am – Tuesday, November 18th
Tiki, Florida

The battered cab, its only identification the placard in the windshield, slowed to a crawl searching for house number 25 on Panda Lane. The driver peered under the passenger doorframe muttering something about inconsiderate bastards who don't put street numbers on their houses.

Penny spotted it first. "There it is!! See it? The sign. TIKI. Pull in the drive."

"Thanks, Miss. That's twenty five bucks."

"Here's thirty; give me your card so I can call you for the return ride." Penny wondered where Sutton was as she pulled her overnighter from the cab.

She needn't have. Drew was halfway down the front path as she slid from the back seat.

"Hi, Penny. What's with the luggage?" Drew smiled and eyed the suitcase. "Staying for awhile?"

"Shut up, Sergeant," she said and planted an affectionate kiss on his mouth. "Take me to your boudoir. Better yet, take me to one of those Polynesian lunches."

Drew smiled and held her at arms length to admire her. She looked somehow radiant.

"You look great," he said, "Missed you. The grill is lit. Hamburger, hot dog or Mahi Mahi?"

"Fish?"

"Yep. Wrapped in cabbage leaves."

Penny ignored him. The house layout, the yard, the inland waterway, the shaded lawn, the pool – she took in all at once and a bit at a time. Her eyes widened with each glance.

"Who owns this place," she asked.

"The Coulters - Art and his wife, Mary Simpson. I thought you might have known Art. He's a retired captain from the department. Headed the Narcotics Squad."

Penny looked at him quizzically. "How long ago?"

"About four years."

Penny's amazement turned to thoughtfulness. "I don't know why, but I hadn't heard of him."

"Look; they have given us free run of the place for a day or two. Let's enjoy it." Drew unwrapped two pieces of fish and placed them on the gas grill.

Lunch was a quiet affair. They quietly enjoyed each other, the food and the Mai Tais. And now they lounged in lawn chairs side by side disengaging their hands occasionally to wave to passing boats. But the question of the Coulters and Drew's presence hung in the air.

"How and why are you here," she asked.

Drew gazed straight ahead and reminded Penny of her role in delivering the note and the events starting at his arrival at Tiki up to the time of her own arrival.

Penny took it all in and digested each word. "Then why am I here," she asked.

Drew twisted in his chair and stared at her unbelievingly. "Because I wanted to see you, to hear you, to smell you, to talk to you. I need to talk to you," he exclaimed. "You didn't need me to tell you this; did you?"

"No. But we could have done this at Lehigh. Why here?"

Drew had no answer. She was right, of course. But his decision had been thought out here and he wanted to tell her here.

"I've been doing a lot of thinking," he said.

"About what," she said apprehensively.

"About me, about what I'm doing, about us."

"What about us?"

"Look, Penny," Drew stammered, "these last few years have been good to me but, frankly, I'm getting tired of being lied to; tired of being shit upon, spat upon; tired of doing business with those cretans in the city. I took this job because Eddy urged me, because Father Pagano spoke for me. It was good while it lasted and I'm grateful for the experience and the good people I've met; I'll miss them but I'm calling it a day."

"Anything else?"

"There's nothing more to say, is there? I've said it all except that I'll be looking for a job teaching somewhere. You know – political science; criminal justice. I really like it and can handle them. What do you think?"

Penny felt a hollow, empty feeling in her stomach. *That's it?* she thought! *Nothing else? What about that word us?* She was expecting a couple of days of romance and intimacy; but this? She wanted to cry but her emotions were frozen in anxiety.

Drew never saw it coming. Penny got up and looked down at Sutton.

"Let me make it easy for you," she muttered. "I'll be packing and going up north as soon as I put my things together." She whirled and left a dumfounded Sutton sitting slack - jawed on the edge of his lounge chair.

Sutton raced after her and pulled her up short by her shoulder. "Hey, what's this all about? What in the hell are you so upset about?"

Doubt and dread clouded her face. "I'm pregnant."

They stood searching each other's face for a reaction. None was forthcoming, their disquieted thoughts masking their feelings.

Drew took Penny by the shoulders and pulled her to him and hugged her. "I don't know why I should be surprised; we had some steamy sessions," he said. "I'm sorry you're upset. Want to talk about it?"

"Not here. Let's walk somewhere; somewhere fresh and mind clearing."

Drew took her to the shoreline and they walked quietly, hand in hand along the water's edge.

Penny spoke first. "I'm scared. I raised one child as a single mother and now another?"

Drew was noncommittal. "I hope for your sake it's a girl. She'll be a happy diversion, a good friend. It'll give Jeff a younger sister to adore and protect. It'll work out. That is, if you want it."

"And you," Penny stopped and stared at Drew. "How do you feel about it all?"

"I'm not going to abandon you, if that's what you mean. I'm not going to run away and hide. I'll help," he said.

Penny reached up and pulled his head down; her lips to his ear. "I'll always love you," she whispered. "This doesn't change my feelings for you."

Drew stood and gazed with affection at the second thing in his life to offer him such commitment and a sense of being. "You are too wonderful."

But their absorption was interrupted by a squinting old seadog.

"Well, bust my barnacles," Holmy Dance cried. "The young cop on the run – or whatever it was you were mooning about. Is this the problem you were having the last time we met?" Dance beamed at Penny. "Hell, man, she's the kind of problem every man should have in his life." And Holmy took her hand and gave it a pleasant squeeze.

"Penny, meet Holmy. I mentioned him this afternoon."

"Holman Dance, Ma'am; at your service. Dammit, Sutton, if I was twenty years younger and she was ten years older, you wouldn't stand a chance." Holmy grinned and winked at Penny.

She laughed at him. "Want to try anyway?"

"Now there's a fun girl. "Mind if I join up with you? Seems you and me went this way before, Drew."

"Do we have a choice?" asked Drew.

"Not as long as you got this mermaid on your arm."

"Where's Jake?"

"Sniffing the briny air someplace. He'll catch up. Seriously, am I intruding?"

They danced away from an incoming wavelet.

"Not really, Holmy; it's good to see you again," responded Drew who was glad for the change of pace. "We were going down to the Clam Bar for an easy gin and tonic. Come along; we'll get to know each other in a different setting. I'm not a bad guy after all."

Holman Dance got between them and put his arms around each waist. "Drew, Penny, I really hope we can meet again. I'll walk you down but Jake will only make a nuisance of himself; me being in the bar without him. I watched you two before I interrupted you. You look good together. Good luck to you both."

And Holman Dance walked away, paused, turned and looked back. He cupped his hands against the breeze and shouted, "And say hello to Tux whoever and wherever he might be." He threw his hands in the air, shook his head dubiously, turned and continued up the shoreline.

Chapter Twenty Four

10:00 am –Friday, November 21ˢᵗ
Elizabeth, New Jersey Police Department

Lt. Traxel leaned back in his chair, hands clasped behind his head and looked across his desk at a humbled Drew Sutton.

"How was the flight up?"

"Nice. Good. Uneventful, no turbulence and on time."

Traxel toyed with the letter on his desk trying to find the appropriate words. "Has this anything to do with the Serfis matter?"

"Not really, I just decided there are other things I'd rather be doing," Sutton replied.

"You know, of course, they collared Alvarez, Martinez, Salinas and company," Traxel spoke softly but firmly.

Drew bolted upright and craned forward. "No, I didn't know. When?"

"About two weeks ago. We gave up Martinez to the Feds but have a detainer on him just in case. We have a municipal corruption investigation going on him. By the way, Salinas was asking for you," Traxel grinned.

Sutton couldn't contain himself. "Great. At least we got something out of this mess."

"What mess? If you hadn't had a hard on for Dalton he'd still be down there and you'd be......"

"Skip it, boss; forget it," Sutton found the memories less than comfortable.

"Now, about this resignation - want to change your mind before I send it up?"

"It's final," Drew said without hesitation.

"Well, at least it will save me some paper work and Internal Affairs appearances," he replied, "Case closed; Sutton gone. Do you want to tell me about it?

"I'm not officially gone yet. Is this off the record?"

"Shoot."

Drew sheepishly laid out the story of Ari and their amours. He became intense when he spoke of their confrontation on the cruise; Hagerty and his leukemia (*wonder where he is now*); Salinas and their surreptitious meeting, the agreement to try to set up Dalton; Coulter – all of it. "Sorry for the bind I put you in."

"Sergeant; Captain Coulter and I are long time friends - went to the academy together. I know Mary well; her stint with DEA. I was right behind you every step of the way. I knew you'd do the right thing sooner or later."

Traxel looked up slowly and deliberately. "How does Eddy fit in?"

Drew looked Traxel in the eye and remained silent.

"Nothing, eh? And Penny Ancebia; what about her?"

"What about her?" Drew bristled.

"I suppose it's just coincidence that she resigned and went to live at her uncle's place in Pennsylvania."

Drew was speechless. "When?"

Eddy Nolan opened the door carrying a brief case filled with Drew's personal property. "Want a ride somewhere, bro?"

Drew turned to Traxel. "The one person who has been left out of all this is Mrs. Chusinsky. I'd like to drop in on her. How about Eddy going with me? I'm sure she'd like to hear from both of us."

"Permission granted. But you didn't answer my question," Traxel smiled knowingly.

He stood up and shook Drew's hand. It was a firm, lingering hand shake of kinship. "Take care, Sergeant. Stay safe. Say Hi to Penny."

%

Mrs. Chusinsky sat quietly in her rocker, a hand-quilted lap robe across her bony knees, her hands on top twirling her thumbs slowly.

"I'm sorry to hear about Mr. Chusinsky," Nolan said, "When did it happen?"

"Not long after. He started drinking more and more," she whispered, "But he was a good man," she added defensively.

Sutton couldn't imagine the emotional trauma this woman had endured. All she ever wanted was a grown family to love and to be loved by; someone to take care of her and her husband in their old age; a simple recompense for being a good Christian person and this was her reward - a dead husband and a murdered junkie son. Drew was reliving his Mother's last years – a good woman of similar and not uncommon circumstance in a life on earth.

"Well," Drew stammered, searching for those right words that are never found. "We kept our promise. We found the man who killed Ben. We thought you would like to know. Maybe there is some peace in that."

"I suppose," she murmured, "Thank you for coming to tell me. Can I make you a cup of coffee?"

"No thank you," Nolan said, "We have some places to go. It's always something for us." There was nothing else to say; nothing that would lighten the load in her heart.

"Good bye, Mrs. Chusinsky." They shook her cold hand and left.

Chapter Twenty Five

Saturday, November 23rd
Lehigh, Pennsylvania

The ride on route 80 seemed extraordinarily long and tedious. Drew wondered how he would approach Penny and Jeff when he got to the campus of Lehigh University. She had said she would meet him there and spend the weekend. He longed for her; her steadfastness, her support, her warmth and her love. And Jeff, that little scamp; a good kid. He liked him and the feelings seemed mutual. Jeff was open and transparent and Drew was certain he had the boy's admiration.

Drew fingered the packet in his jacket pocket. *What will Penny think; what will she say?*

Penny sat fidgeting on the living room couch of her uncle's home while Jeff stared at the fire in the fireplace mesmerized by the dancing, multicolored flames. The clock cuckooed six. Drew was later than she had hoped. She tried to form her sentences in several ways – *Hello, Drew; good to see you* – no good. *Hi sweetie, you look great. How did it go* – no good. How about – *Jeff and I are so glad you're here* – not much better.

Dammit, Drew, where are you? Her anxiety started to take hold. *Damn, I miss him so.*

Tires sounded like popping walnuts in the graveled drive and Jeff leaped to his feet, "He's here, Mom, he's here."

Drew flung open the door.

"Hello, Pen. Come here, Jeff. I'm home."

Penny ran to him but Jeff got there first. "Hey, hey," shouted Drew, "one at a time." But it meant nothing. Jeff was pinned between them and they laughed.

Penny ran to the kitchen and came back with two glasses. How about slipping out of those wet clothes and into a dry martini," she joked.

"Great. Jeff, there are two bags in the back of the car. Get them for me, please."

"Aye, aye," he saluted and ran to the car.

The "hellos" and "how are yous" quieted and the fire place emanated a soft warmth. Jeff had gone reluctantly to bed and Drew and Penny sat before the fire glow quietly enjoying each other.

"How will your interview with the Political Science Department go?"

"Piece of cake. I got tentative approval over the phone two days ago."

"Will I have to call you Professor?"

"Adjunct."

"I don't care much for 'I love you, Adjunct.'"

Penny sat up on the couch and faced Drew. "Speaking of things – who is this person, Tux, Holmy was talking about the other day?"

Drew dodged the subject. "Speaking of things," he interjected, "I have something for you," and he pulled a 2" square velvet box from his pocket.

Penny smiled and held her face to his. "Is this what I think it is?"

"Damn, Pen; open it before I lose my nerve."

"The answer is yes, yes, yes," she cried without opening the box. "I just hope you will be as happy as I am now."

"Yay," yelled Jeff standing in the open bedroom doorway. "Mom said we might be together."

Drew luxuriated in the affection of their conspiracy.

"We'll need a home of our own. We can't stay here forever."

"Let not your heart be troubled, kind sir," Penny said, "Uncle Cal will be moving to the University of North Carolina in the spring. He says we can stay here if you get the job. And the rent will be dirt cheap – enough to meet an adjunct's pay."

"Penny," Drew looked from one to the other, "If this is love, I'll take a ton."

"It's love and family, all of us, and I mean all of us - here and to be. I love you dearly."

Yet Penny would not be put off. "Tell us about Tux. Is he someone I should know?"

"Who's Tux," Jeff, now back from his bedroom, looked from one to the other.

Drew took in a breath, paused and looked at the ceiling, trying to find a starting point. He set Jeff on his lap.

"Penny," he said, "there was this sea-gull who seemed to appear at the oddest moments while I was working the Chusinsky case. He was black and white which made him look as if he were wearing a tuxedo."

"That's it? A sea-gull?"

"Do you want to hear this or not?"

"Go on."

"Well, the first time I saw him he was flying circles around me at the Kill. I saw him again in New York, screeching and wheeling around in the air; and again in Art Coulter's back yard – same thing: squealing and squawking at me. Yes, at me. No doubt about it. The next time I saw him was when Dalton's body washed up. It was like a dance he was doing on his body. And when Holmy and I approached, he flew around me, again screeching and squealing, flying circles around me until he finally flew off."

"That's weird," Penny said.

"That's what Holmy said – words to that effect. Anyway, Bruce Springsteen wrote lyrics to a song about a young Lieutenant on the road to Basra that goes something like this –

"At night he dreams he sees their souls rise
like dark geese to the Oklahoma skies."

Penny felt her skin crawl. "And you think this …this Tux is, or was, Ben Chusinsky's soul; is that it?"

"Yes."

"Yikes," yelled Jeff and jumped from Drew's lap and ran off to bed.

"And you, Penny; do you think you can you live with this?" asked Drew.

"I've thought that for years," she said, took his hand and led him from the couch. "Come on, sweetheart; bed time."

Epilogue

In Memoriam:

<u>Dead Benny</u>

My real name is Benny Chusinsky
Big Ben to those in the know
I was once a fun-loving guy
Now caught in the bay's undertow.

I really don't know how it happened
It was vicious and fast, the attack
The knife flashed in rhythmic succession
As it plunged in my chest then my back.

The bar had closed early that morning
To keep in step with the law
But me and my friends were still drinkin'
And started to talk and to jaw.

Big Al was the tavern's new owner
Tough with a shadowy past
His drinks and strip dancers well known
As well as his coke and his grass

Now, I'd done him quite a few favors
An entrepreneur so to speak
Sold some of his junk to outsiders
Owed him the dough from last week.

Last night he wanted the money
But I was not able to pay
He didn't think that was too funny
And quickly ended my day.

So now I drift much like the flotsam
Upon life's turbulent sea
Wrapped tight in his bloody blanket
Floating with all the debris.

I hope they nail the bastard
I was really a fun lovin' guy
To be treated like this is uncalled for
I was only a coupla grand shy.

Tux

About the Author

The author is a retired Prosecutor's Detective Sergeant with twenty years experience in the investigation of homicides and the cause and manner of sudden deaths, the realm of the occult, suicides both real and disguised, and sex crimes.

About the Book

When detective Sergeant Andrew Sutton found himself without a clue in the murder of Ben Chusinsky, he decided to take justice by the hand but instead found himself the object of a search by his department and a drug money laundering network with tentacles reaching South America. His dalliance with a medical examiner almost ruined a career that was saved by the conspiracy of his partner and a woman who loved him.

Only coincidence and luck brought resolution to a case that had produced a floating body lacking in forensics, a crime scene that had been quickly sold out from under the investigation, and the death of a greedy murderer whose demise was greeted with cheers by the anguished soul of the victim.